Ask the CARDS A QUESTION

A Sharon McCone Mystery

Marcia Muller

G.K. Hall & Co.
Thorndike, Maine

Published in 1996 by arrangement with
Aaron Priest M. Literary Agency, Inc.

G.K. Hall Large Print Paperback Collection.

The text of this Large Print edition is unabridged.
Other aspects of the book may vary from the original edition.

Set in 16 pt. News Plantin by Minnie B. Raven.

Printed in the United States on permanent paper.

Library of Congress Cataloging in Publication Data

Muller, Marcia.
    Ask the cards a question : a Sharon McCone mystery / Marcia Muller.
        p.   cm.
    ISBN 0-7838-1480-1 (lg. print : lsc)
    1. McCone, Sharon (Fictitious character) — Fiction. 2. Private investigators — California — San Francisco — Fiction. 3. Women detectives — California — San Francisco — Fiction. 4. San Francisco (Calif.) — Fiction. 5. Large type books. I. Title.
    [PS3563.U397A9   1996]
    813'.54—dc20   95-45118

CA
A

Also published in Large Print
from G.K. Hall by Marcia Muller:

Trophies and Dead Things
Games to Keep the Dark Away
Leave a Message for Willie
The Cheshire Cat's Eye

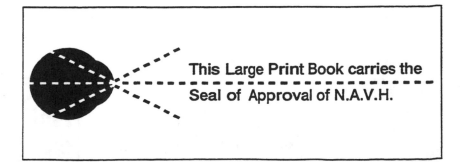

For Sue Dunlap

1

I circled the block in my noisy old MG, senses alert and ready for action. Nothing.

Another block, and still another. My frustration deepened. I'd give anything for . . . a parking space!

With a clash of gears, the car and I hurtled backwards into the spot. At last, after five hours overtime and a twenty-five minute search for this space, I was free to walk four and a half blocks through the darkness to my apartment.

Still, it wasn't a bad night for a walk. San Francisco weather was unpredictable in April, but this year we had had sun-washed days and mild evenings. I strolled toward Guerrero Street, the breeze banishing my aggravation.

Around the corner, red lights pulsated, their waves shattering the darkness. I stopped outside their range. Police cars. Crowds of onlookers. In front of my building. Panic shot through me, and I ran.

Linnea, I thought. Linnea. Shouldn't have left her alone so long. Talked about suicide . . . a lot . . . since the divorce . . . all her drinking . . . God knows what kind of pills . . . my best friend . . . comes to me for help . . . I

7

leave her alone . . . in there . . . drinking . . . day after day.

The crowd seemed a solid mass. I pushed through.

"Hey, lady, don't shove!"

"What's happened in there? What's happened?"

"Somebody died."

"Dead body."

"Oh, my God!"

"Hey, quit shoving!"

Sternly, a young patrolman barred my way. "Sorry ma'am. You can't go in there."

I sidestepped, but he blocked me.

"Sorry, ma'am," he repeated.

"I *live* here, dammit!"

Confused, he hesitated. I ran up the steps to the lobby.

A crowd of residents milled about, two more uniformed officers holding them at bay from the stairway. Immediately I glanced at the door of my first-floor rear apartment. It was closed, and no light shone through the pebbled-glass panes.

A bulky figure loomed in front of the table near the stairway. Tim O'Riley, the building manager. In the dim rays of the lobby chandelier, Tim's normally ruddy face was ashen, and his mouth hung slack. His thick fingers, unaccustomed to being without a can of beer, played nervously with the heap of advertising circulars and junk mail on the table.

I put my hand on his arm.

"Tim, what's going on?"

8

He started. "Oh, it's you. Jeez, Sharon, something awful's happened."

"I know. Someone died. Who?"

"Mrs. Antonio." His puffy face twisted with grief.

So my friend was all right! And this was death of natural causes. Molly Antonio, one of the second-floor tenants, was in her sixties and had a history of heart trouble. "Heart attack, huh?"

Tim shook his head and passed a hand over his bloodshot eyes. "Worse. Lots worse. Somebody killed her."

"Good Lord!" I spun around, almost colliding with one of the patrolmen. "Who's in charge here?" I demanded.

He stared impassively at me. Older and more seasoned than the first officer, he was not about to let a pushy woman bother him. "We'll get to you people in a while."

"Terrific." I turned back to Tim and, lowering my voice, asked, "Have you seen Linnea?"

"Not for a few hours." He looked at his watch. "Last I saw her, she was lugging this big jug of wine into your apartment. That was maybe around five. Then the stereo started playing real loud — you know how she'll do that — but it's been quiet for probably an hour. She must be stinko by now."

"Thank God."

Tim looked shocked. I had to admit it was an odd reaction to my friend drinking herself into oblivion.

"What I mean is that she's been spared all this." I gestured around the lobby. "Molly Antonio was particularly kind to her. Linnea's going to take her death hard."

Tim nodded sagely. "And if she was conscious, she'd be having hysterics all over the place."

I didn't want to talk about my friend's nervous breakdown just now. "One thing you can do for me, Tim."

"Sure."

"Unless the police ask, don't tell them she's staying with me. They'd insist on waking her up, and . . ."

"I get it."

"Thanks." I pressed his arm and turned back, determined to find out who was in charge.

Again the patrolman blocked me, looking more bored than annoyed. "Ma'am, you will just have to wait."

I was formulating a statement that would produce results when a big man in a tan trenchcoat appeared on the stairway. Lieutenant Greg Marcus, of the SFPD Homicide Squad. He loped down the steps, casually brushing his blond hair from his forehead.

"Greg," I called.

He didn't hear me.

"Gregory!"

The patrolman's eyes widened. Normal citizens didn't screech in such a manner at Homicide detectives.

Greg whirled. "Sharon!" He hurried over and

10

slipped his arm around my shoulders. The patrolman sighed resignedly and turned away.

"I'm ashamed of you," Greg said. "A murder happens in your very own building, and when I arrive on the scene, you're not even home. You did just get here, right?"

I nodded.

"Well, that's pretty slipshod of you. A truly dedicated private eye would have found the body herself."

I smiled weakly, feeling drained.

"Hey, what's happened to the old McCone bravado?" Greg asked. "You're not letting a little murder and mayhem shake you?"

I knew the men on Homicide were hardened characters and that jokes were not uncommon at the crime scene, but such behavior didn't fit with my conception of Greg. My face must have reflected the thought, because he sobered instantly.

"Sorry. It's the only way I can keep the job from getting to me," he said. "Was the victim a friend of yours?"

"You could say she was a friend of everyone who lives here." It was true. In this highly transient and impersonal building in the Mission District, Molly was the one who baked cookies at Christmas, watered plants for vacationing tenants, and took in packages from the postman so they wouldn't be stolen. She, along with a handful of others, brought warmth to an urban life that was too often chilled by indifference, hostility,

11

and crime. I would miss her.

"Well, right now I can use your help." Greg's arm tightened around my shoulders, and he led me toward the stairs.

"Wait a minute. Where are we going?"

"I need an ID on the body from someone who's reasonably sane and sober. The husband's hysterical, the manager's a boozer, and most of your fellow tenants don't look any too straight either. So, papoose, it's up to you."

"Oh, great." I grimace at the nickname, which was Greg's tribute to my one-eighth American Indian ancestry, and at the task ahead. We started for the stairs. "Did Gus find her?"

"The husband? Yes. Around eleven, when he came back from playing dominoes at the corner bar."

"Ellen T's," I said mechanically.

"Right. He fell apart, and we had to call a doctor — they're in the manager's apartment." Greg stopped on the landing and leaned against the wall. His dark-blond eyebrows were drawn together in displeasure, and the shadows elongated his face. "Sharon, there's something strange about this setup."

"What do you mean?"

"The husband — Gus — keeps raving about how he always comes here for coffee and cake — *before* going home."

"Oh." I nodded. "I guess it would sound odd if you didn't know them. Gus is — was — married to Molly, but she couldn't stand to live with him.

12

So, for the past five years, he's had his own place up the hill on Twenty-second Street, but he eats all his meals with Molly and comes over every night for a snack when he finishes his domino game."

Greg frowned. "Sharon, why do you live in such a weird building?"

"No, listen. Molly claimed it was a perfectly sensible arrangement. She said a wife has a duty to cook for her man and keep his clothes clean, but that there was no reason to be driven completely crazy on account of him. She may have had a point."

Greg continued up the stairs. "I'm glad I didn't marry someone like Molly," he said over his shoulder. "And remind me to quit pursuing you, if that's your way of thinking." At the top, he added, "Not that I've had much luck with my pursuit lately."

"No, you haven't."

He turned to face me, frowning. "Sharon, isn't it time we made peace?"

I felt all my defenses rise against him. "Right now we have other things to think about." As I spoke, I glanced at the stairway to the third floor, where yet another officer held back a group of residents. On the top step stood a gaunt, hatchet-faced woman with gray-streaked black hair pulled back in a bun. Mrs. Neverman, a close friend of Molly's. Her dark eyes were wet and shimmering in the light of the orange bulb on the landing.

Greg's gaze had followed mine. He dropped a hand onto my shoulder. "Shall we go in?"

The door to the second-floor front apartment stood open, a shaft of light falling across the turquoise carpet in the hall. A hum of voices came from within. I hung back. Greg guided me forward, and reluctantly, I stepped over the threshold.

Just inside, on the little telephone stand that Molly had found at a garage sale and lovingly refinished, lay a bag of groceries, its contents spilling over onto the floor. The phone had been knocked off the hook. I stepped around a package of frozen lima beans and went into the living room, where lab technicians were at work.

Molly's sheeted figure lay in the center of the room, on a blue rug Greg went over and lifted a corner of the covering. Her face, beneath her coif of white hair, was deeply purpled. I could see the mark where something — a wire? a fine cord? — had bitten into her throat.

I nodded and turned away. "It's Molly."

Greg came up behind me. "Thanks."

"Don't mention it. Was it robbery, do you know?" My voice was thick and shook slightly.

"A very strange robbery, if that."

"How so?"

"I'll show you." He led me to the bedroom. The drawers of the dresser had been pulled out, lingerie and stockings scattered on the floor. "Whoever it was went through the closet and the kitchen drawers, too," Greg said, "but he didn't touch the jewelry box or the TV, or a metal lockbox sitting right out in plain sight on the desk."

"A robbery with a specific purpose, then."

"Very specific."

We went back to the living room. "Did you find the murder weapon?" I asked.

Greg picked up a plastic evidence bag from the end table. I started when I saw the coiled length of white drapery cord. It looked like the extra segment I had cut off when I'd threaded the rod for my new curtains just the other day. Of course, all pieces of cord looked alike. Mine was probably still lying on the coffee table where I'd left it. Or was it? And if not . . .

Greg frowned. "Papoose, are you all right?"

"Yes. No. Oh, this whole thing is so . . ." I gestured helplessly and started for the door. In the hall of the apartment, a sudden rush of tears stung my eyes and, to cover it, I knelt to examine the spilled groceries.

"Looks like she came in from shopping and surprised her killer," Greg said.

A cash register receipt hearing the imprint of the Albatross Superette lay among the apples and oranges and cracked eggs. I pointed to it. "That's the ma and pa store down the block. Their prices are high, so I don't shop there much, just for things I forget to pick up at Safeway. But Molly didn't have a car, and I suppose she had to buy most of her groceries there."

Greg grunted. "That's the plight of the urban

15

poor. Forced to pay rip-off prices for the sake of convenience."

"Well, I don't suppose your average neighborhood grocer's volume is high enough that he can afford to charge less either." Gingerly, I poked the frozen lima beans. The package was beaded with moisture but still firm.

"You know the time of death yet?" I stood up.

"Just a range. After six, before ten. We'll have a better idea after the postmortem."

"Will you let me know?"

"Sure. But why the interest?"

"Let's just say this hits pretty close to home."

"I understand. Why don't you give me a call tomorrow afternoon." With a wicked gleam in his eye, he added, "It'll give me a chance to continue my pursuit of you."

I made a face at him and started out. His voice stopped me.

"What's that noise?"

A faint growling, obscured until now by the activity around us, came from the living room.

"Oh, Lord!" I exclaimed. "It's Watney!"

"Watney?"

"Molly's cat." I went back and dragged the fat black-and-white cat from under the sofa, receiving a long scratch for my efforts. Once out, the creature burrowed into my arms, head tucked into the crook of my elbow. "I'd better take him down to my place."

Greg nodded. "Talk to you later."

I carried the cowering animal downstairs and through the dwindling crowd, hefting him with difficulty while I fished out my keys and opened the door. Inside, I released him, and he made a beeline for the main room.

I followed, turning on a table lamp as I entered. In the bed by the window of my combination living room and bedroom was a woman-size lump with a shock of wheat-colored hair. My friend, Linnea Carraway. A wine jug stood empty on the floor beside her, the sweet odor of sauterne permeating the air. Linnea exuded its aroma.

Not only had she passed out, but she'd done so in my bed.

With a flash of annoyance, I put my hand on her shoulder and shook her. She didn't respond.

Alarmed, I felt for her pulse. It was steady. Linnea was merely suffering the effects of drinking over half a gallon of cheap wine.

I let go of her arm, resisting the impulse to pinch her. The stereo was still on, faint crackling noises coming from its speakers. I flipped the switch off and eyed Watney, who was inspecting the sleeping bag on the floor, where Linnea should have been.

Conscious of my stare, the cat flattened himself and disappeared under the bed. I decided to leave him there and get some sleep. As I slipped into the bag, telling myself I should pretend I was on a fun camping trip, a sudden thought hit me.

I got back up and went over to the coffee table between the matching easy chairs.

The length of white drapery cord was gone.

2

I crossed the street toward the Albatross Superette, morning sun warm on my shoulders and
a sense of guilt hot at my heels.

Linnea hadn't stirred as I dressed hastily that
morning. I knew I should have awakened her
to tell her of Molly's murder; it would be far
better for her to hear of it from me than from
the TV news or someone like Tim, the manager.
Still, after a restless night on the floor, I was
in no shape to face her probable hysterics, and
I'd taken the coward's way out.

Or was that the real reason I'd slunk out of
my own apartment without so much as a cup
of coffee? What about the length of drapery cord
which, I was sure, had traveled from my place
to the scene of Molly's death? How do you ask
your best friend if she, by any chance, wandered
upstairs in a drunken stupor and strangled an
old lady? How on earth can you even think such
a thing?

I shook off the thought and opened the door
of the Superette, sniffing the aroma of coffee from
the big urn the proprietor always kept going.
The little store was empty. I stepped inside, taking
in the familiar Coca-Cola and bubbling neon beer

signs, the worn green-and-white linoleum and battered freezer chests, the racks of potato chips and neat pyramids of fresh fruit.

A dour-faced man with oil-slicked black hair emerged from the stockroom. He wiped his hands on his long white apron and came forward. "You have heard the news, Miss McCone?" His words were accentuated not so much by his native Arabic tongue as by excessive formality.

"You mean about Molly Antonio? Yes."

"A terrible thing. A truly terrible thing." Briefly, he bowed his head, then slipped around me and turned the sign in the window to CLOSED. Locking the door, he added, "I do not wish to speak of such a thing in front of my customers. You would like coffee, perhaps?"

"That sounds good."

He filled two Styrofoam cups and scrupulously rang up the price, depositing change from his own pocket. I sat on a wooden stool next to the counter, watching him and thinking back to five years ago, when I'd first met Mohammed Makhlouf, or Mr. Moe, as he was called.

The first time I'd ever come into the store, I'd gotten a loaf of bread and approached the counter in time to observe the grocer close in on a neophyte delinquent bent on stealing from the candy jar by the cash register. The would-be offender took one look at Mr. Moe's deep-set eyes and upraised hand and backed toward the door. In a flurry of arms and legs, he vanished.

"If you frighten them enough, they will learn,"

Mr. Moe said. He rang up the bread, made change, and offered me a paper bag, which I declined. As I left, he called out after me:

"Thank you for saving the trees!"

Although on the surface a friendly expression of appreciation from one ecologist to another, the remark — and countless others directed at me over the intervening years — had contained an undertone of mockery, accentuated by a thin smile that never touched his eyes. As time went by, my inability to pinpoint the source of this scorn had filled me with a wary curiosity that persisted to this day.

Now Mr. Moe handed me coffee and leaned against the counter, cup between his slender hands. The store was silent, save for the whir of an overhead fan. After a minute, the grocer asked, "You were at home when they found Mrs. Antonio?"

"I arrived right afterwards. Gus was hysterical, so I identified the body."

"And why would the police permit a pretty young woman like you to view such a horror?" His characteristic irony colored the words.

"My job makes me tougher than I look. I'm a private detective, with All Souls Legal Cooperative, the legal services plan."

"A detective?" Something flickered in the pools of the grocer's eyes and his lids, almost lashless, slid down, lending his face a faintly reptilian cast.

"That's right." I watched him closely.

"I did not know." He set his coffee down untouched and began to straighten some brushes hanging from a display rack beside him. A sign on top of the rack read: THESE PRODUCTS MANUFACTURED AT THE SUNRISE BLIND CENTER . . . HELP THE BLIND HELP THEMSELVES.

"The morning news said a burglar invaded Mrs. Antonio's home and killed her," Mr. Moe went on. "What could she have worth stealing?"

So that was the story the police had given the press. "Not much," I said. "Did you know her well?"

"I knew her, yes. There are many old ladies like Mrs. Antonio in the neighborhood. They come in here every day. I cash their Social Security checks, extend them credit at the end of the month. We are as close to friends as is possible in a place like this." His gesture took in all of the Mission District, maybe all of San Francisco.

I asked, "What time did Molly come in here last night?"

His hooded glance slid sidelong toward me. "Why would you think she did?"

"She spilled her bag of groceries, probably when she was attacked. I saw your cash register receipt."

"I see. Yes." He left off the brushes and turned to face me, his arms folded across his white-aproned chest. "Miss McCone, I did not mean to be untruthful. I am afraid for my business. That she was here immediately before she was killed. . . ."

"You say immediately before. How do you know when she died?"

His tongue darted out, licking at his dry lips. "That is a figure of speech. Minutes or hours, what is the difference?"

"It could be important. You may have been the last person to see her alive. What time was it?"

"Perhaps seven o'clock. I did not look at the time."

"How did she seem? Was she in good spirits?"

"She was the same as before."

"Before?"

"Yes. At five o'clock, she stopped in and asked me to tell Gus to come to her place when he brought Sebastian, the blind brush man, in here. She wanted him to be sure to see her before he returned Sebastian to the Blind Center." Mr. Moe gestured at the rack. Sebastian, the brush man, lived at the Sunrise Blind Center, a few blocks away. Led by Molly's husband, Gus, he traveled about the neighborhood restocking the vending racks in various grocery stores. The Center paid Gus a small salary in return for acting as guide.

"Okay. How did she seem then?" I asked.

"She was upset. Agitated. I asked her what was wrong."

"And?"

"She laughed and tried to make nothing of it. She said she had received an evil prophecy from her fortune teller."

"Her fortune teller? What on earth?"

23

"Mrs. Antonio, like many of the foolish old ladies around here, went once a week to a fortune teller. She took it very seriously."

"For heaven's sake. Who is this person?"

The grocer hesitated. "Fortune telling is illegal here, so they keep their identities secret. They use flyers and word of mouth, advertising as 'Madame So-and-so.' The city is full of these prophetesses and faith healers."

"And you don't know which one Molly went to?"

Again he hesitated. I sensed he wanted to protect the fortune teller. "No," he said. "Surely you don't think a prophecy killed Mrs. Antonio?"

"Of course not. But it's interesting. I never would have taken Molly for a superstitious woman. She seemed so down-to-earth."

A rapping at the door broke the silence. The grocer went over and opened it, turning the sign back around. Two truckers from the Produce Terminal stood there, eager to make their deliveries.

I tossed my empty cup in the trash can and stood up. "Oh, by the way, Mr. Moe." My voice sounded thin and evasive.

"Yes?"

"Do you know my friend, Linnea Carraway? She's about five-three, with long blond hair."

"The lady who buys all the wine." His face was a polite blank.

"Yes, that's the one. Was she in yesterday?" Since Linnea had drunk wine last night, rather

24

than the Scotch she preferred, she'd probably bought it locally. The stores in the surrounding blocks only stocked beer and wine.

"Yes," Mr. Moe replied. "She bought some wine immediately before Mrs. Antonio arrived. In fact, Mrs. Antonio scolded her for it. She told her to run along home and she'd stop in later for a chat."

I stood, staring at him.

"Is that all, Miss McCone? I have a great deal of work to do."

"Oh, of course. Thank you for your time."

I threaded my way through the deliverymen and crates on the sidewalk, thinking I would need to have a chat with Linnea, too. As I reached the curb, I spotted Greg Marcus on the opposite corner. He waved and came toward me, jaunty in his blue pin-striped suit. We met in the center of the street.

"Looks like you're ahead of me, papoose. Find out anything interesting?"

"Me?" I widened my eyes, miming innocence. "All I did was have a cup of coffee."

"Sure you did. Just coffee and conversation. I'll get back to you later."

3

I shoved the stand that held my old Underwood portable into a corner of my office. Eleven o'clock. The report I'd worked on all yesterday evening and part of this morning was finally done.

The red push-button phone on my desk buzzed softly. I punched the flashing button and picked up the receiver.

"Well, papoose," Greg's voice greeted me, "will you give me my big chance and have lunch with me today?"

As they had the night before, my defenses rose. "I plan to catch a bite here and work on my expense report."

"Ah, Sharon, how unromantic! It's too beautiful a day for such nonsense, and the good weather can't last much longer. Come on a picnic with me."

I hesitated. Greg and I had met on a case two months ago and had instantly become professional rivals. We had then begun to work on becoming friends, a tough uphill job, given our respective stormy natures and the traditional antagonism that exists between cops and private eyes. Six weeks ago, after a quarrel, I had decided things could never work out for us, and Greg, with characteristic determination, had proceeded to try to woo me back. So far I had resisted.

"Come on. Please."

"Will you promise not to bring any chocolate?" Unlike other men, who would ply a woman with flowers, Greg had been showering me with chocolate — for which we both had a fondness bordering on the obsessive.

"Me? Why would I bring any of that along?"

"Greg, really. After that box of See's fudge two days ago I've had about all I can take." It had been on the doorsteps when I'd returned from work.

"Ate it all, eh?"

"Well . . ."

"Listen, papoose, why don't you stop at the deli near All Souls and pick up some beer and sandwiches? Then come down here and liberate me from my paperwork."

I sighed. It *was* a beautiful day and, as Greg had said, the good weather couldn't hold much longer. "Okay. What time?"

"Can you wait until one? I'll have the results of the PM on Antonio by then."

It was a bribe. I agreed and hung up.

With two empty hours on my hands, I wandered down the hall to the front desk where Ted, the paralegal worker, rattled away on his Selectric. While not new, it beat my Underwood, and I coveted it, although I realized both the volume and the quality of my typing did not justify such a machine.

"Where's Hank?" I asked when Ted looked up.

He jerked a thumb at the ceiling. "In bed, pretending to be sick. I think he's actually taking a mental-health day."

It surprised me. My boss, Hank Zahn, seldom took even the vacation time he was entitled to. "If he's only playing possum, I'd like to see him."

"Don't think he'll mind. Go on up."

I climbed to the second floor of the big Victorian that housed All Souls. Several attorneys lived there, in the free rooms that were partial compensation for the low salaries a legal services plan paid. I knocked on the door at the rear, and Hank's voice called out a welcome.

My boss was ensconced in a king-sized bed, surrounded by books, papers and magazines. He leaned against a heap of pillows, his light-brown Brillo pad of hair tousled, a pencil tucked behind one ear.

"Come in, come in." He waved me toward a chair near the bed.

"Is it contagious?"

"Nope. At first I thought it was food poisoning, but now I realize it's due to the poor quality of my cooking. I made this curry last night, and it's lucky nobody ate it but me."

"Ted suspects you're really taking a mental-health day."

"The little fox could be right."

I sat down, staring at Hank's pajamas. They

were white, with little red pigs all over them. Peering closer, I made out the monogram under each. "MCP?"

Hank glanced down, then took off his thick, horn-rimmed glasses and polished them on a flowing sleeve. "Yeah. A gift from a lady friend. Funny, I didn't think I gave the impression of being a chauvinist."

"I think it's a joke."

"Maybe. I can never tell with this particular friend." He gestured at the newspapers near the foot of the bed. "I see you had trouble at your building last night."

"We sure did."

"Friend of yours?"

"Someone I was fond of."

"Greg show up?" Hank and Greg were old friends, from long before I'd known either of them.

"Yes," I said shortly, hoping to forestall a discussion of my love life which, for some reason, fascinated Hank.

"You still pissed off at him?"

I sighed. "I am not, as you so inelegantly put it, pissed off. I merely came to the decision that the relationship would not work."

"After you had a big fight with him."

"Who told you that?"

"No one needed to. I know you."

Besides being my boss, Hank was one of my best friends; he knew me better than most people. "Okay, so we had a fight."

He put on his fatherly expression. "Tell me about it."

There was no way around the issue. Hank, with the skill of years in the courtroom, would get it out of me one way or the other. And I felt safe confiding in him, knowing it would go no further. "It came about very innocently. I was quoting to him from a magazine article about that private eye who had bugged his own testimony before a Senate judiciary committee hearing on electronic eavesdropping. I thought it a clever way to make one's point, but Greg didn't see the humor. He launched into a diatribe against my profession, and you know what kind of response that brought from me. When we got down to personals, I decided it was time to leave."

Hank scratched his curly head. "Shar, you and Greg argue all the time. It's your nature; you both thrive on it."

"I'm not sure I need to thrive that much."

"He wants to make up, you know."

"I know. I've got an apartment full of candy to prove it. He even gave me a foot-tall chocolate bunny he found in a post-Easter sale."

Hank chuckled. "So why not give in?"

"No. We can't be friends unless we respect each other's work."

"And he doesn't respect yours?"

"No."

"Well, it's your life." Hank rummaged around in the bed and came up with a roll of Lifesavers. I shook my head when he offered one to me, wondering what other objects the bed contained. The long red cord of one of the push-button phones that were an All Souls tradition snaked out from under the covers.

"You come up here to sympathize with me, or do you have an ulterior motive?" Hank asked, chomping on the Lifesaver.

"As a matter of fact, I wanted to check on what you have lined up for me."

He scratched his head. "You finished with the report on *DeYoe versus Treakle?*"

"Yes, about half an hour ago."

"Then that's it for now. Things are quiet — all our clients must be dead or minding their own business."

"I suspect the latter." The subscribers to the legal services plan were a placid lot. The report I'd just finished concerned a breach of contract over the installation of a redwood hot tub, a classy commodity for one of our clients.

"Well," Hank said, "why don't you take off and track down this Mrs. Antonio's killer?"

My lips parted in surprise.

"Well, that's what this visit is really about, right?"

Grudgingly, I nodded. "I'm not so sure it's good for a boss to know his employee so well."

"Good or not, I do. Take a couple of vacation days, if you like. I'll be in touch if we need you."

"There goes my vacation again." I sighed.

"It's a worthy cause. I can see you're upset about the murder."

More upset than I dare tell you. "Thanks. Maybe I'll do it."

"Maybe, nothing. You'll do it. Now get out of here and let me suffer in peace."

As I came downstairs, Ted signaled that I had a call. I followed one of the red cords down the hall until I located a phone on a bookcase. I'd often suspected that the folks at All Souls favored twenty-five-foot cords so they could abandon the instruments in peculiar places.

Linnea's hysterical voice assaulted my ear. "Sharon! Sharon, you won't believe what Tim just told me!"

"I already know, Linnea. I was planning to call you."

"Call me? You couldn't tell me in person? I assume you came home last night."

"You're right, I did come home. But I had to go out early, and I didn't want to disturb you."

"Didn't want to disturb me? You think I'm not disturbed now? Being told about a murder by that grinning, leering tub of guts?"

"Linnea, that's no way to talk about Tim."

"I'll talk any way I please! Oh, my God, Sharon! Molly said the cards were to blame. The fortune teller . . ." She began to sob.

Molly had evidently taken the prophecy seriously. "Look, Linnea, I know how you feel. I feel terrible myself. I'm going to talk to the police. . . ."

"The police!"

Her shriek made me hold the receiver away from my ear. "Well, to Greg Marcus. You know — the cop who sends me all the chocolate, the one you've never met."

"What good is that going to do?"

"I'll find out what they know so far."

"And, in the meantime, what do I do?"

"I don't understand."

"Here I sit, in your crummy apartment, all cooped up and scared to death!"

The reference to my apartment stung, but I controlled my voice. "Look, Linnea, why don't you get out of there? Go for a walk. It's a beautiful day."

"Go for a walk, with a maniac on the loose? Are you crazy?"

I sighed. "Okay, do what you like. I'll be home as soon as I can get there. Maybe I'll have some news by then."

"Oh, great!"

"And Linnea, try not to . . ." I paused.

"Try not to what?"

I had been about to tell her not to hit the bottle again, but I knew it would only provoke another outburst. "Try not to worry," I finished lamely.

"Oh, sure." There was a click, and the line went dead.

I set the phone down and leaned against the bookcase, thinking. Linnea's hysteria seemed genuine, not the reaction of someone with something to hide. The problem was, how much did she remember of what she did when drunk? She had confessed to alcoholic blackouts in recent weeks.

"Something has to be done about this situation," I said aloud. "Something has got to be done."

4

At one o'clock I pulled up in front of the massive stone block that was the Hall of Justice. I watched as Greg ambled down the steps, admiring his trim body which, at forty-two, was still fit as an athlete's. Greg was good company, good looking, and, in Hank's words, managed to piss me off totally on the average of once a week.

"Good afternoon." Greg opened the car door and got in. Quickly he reached into his coat pocket and tossed a bag of Hershey Kisses in my lap.

"Dammit! You promised!"

"I did nothing of the kind."

"I'll get fat."

"Good. Then you'll have to start seeing me again because no one else will have you."

I sighed and pulled away from the curb.

"Where are you taking me, by the way?" Greg asked.

"I thought we'd try Dolores Park." I named the grassy slope across from Mission High School.

"That's fine with me. If I really cared, I could probably nab a few dope pushers during lunch. But that would mean more paperwork."

"And I know how you hate paperwork." I shot through a space between a MUNI bus and a police

35

car and headed back toward my own neighborhood.

The park was dotted with loungers, many of them shirtless, spread-eagled to receive the warm rays. Teenaged couples from the school strolled about in ambulatory embraces whose maintenance required ballet-like precision. As we spread my car blanket at the top of the hill, Greg said:

"Ah, if only you would walk in lockstep and talk of love with me!"

I laughed. Greg's bantering had begun to ease the tension I'd felt over this, our first real time together since our quarrel. I sensed he wouldn't press the issue seriously today.

We finished arranging the blanket, and Greg burrowed through the bag from the deli, giving enthusiastic thanks for his salami and cheese sandwich. I opened the two bottles of San Miguel beer and unwrapped my own hot pastrami.

"The lunch is in exchange for information on Molly Antonio's postmortem," I said. "How close were you able to pinpoint the time of death?"

"Very. We know, from the husband, exactly when and what she had for dinner. From the stomach contents, she had to have been killed less than two hours after they ate at six o'clock."

I thought of Gus Antonio, an arthritic little man who seemed continually bewildered by the world around him. "Can you be sure his information is reliable?"

"Reasonably. He and his wife always ate at six on the dot. And the meal stood out in his mind because it was, for her, a particularly sketchy dinner."

"What was it?"

"Hamburgers and fried potatoes. No vegetable, which was strange because she usually insisted on two, even though the husband hates the sight of them. She told him she'd forgotten to shop, but would lay in fresh supplies later."

It fit with what Mr. Moe had told me. "She must have been preoccupied with something, if she'd forgotten to buy vegetables. So, after this sketchy meal — which, incidentally, sounds a lot better than most of mine — Gus went to Ellen T's to play dominoes?"

"Right. He claims he was in the back room all evening, until just before he found the body at eleven. We checked with the bartender, but unfortunately there's a rear exit, by the restrooms. It's possible Gus could have slipped out and come back, on the pretext of going to the john. We're talking to the domino players today, but it's difficult rounding them up."

"It's hard for me to picture Gus doing anything so devious," I said. "He has so much trouble coping with life as is."

"I know what you mean. I had difficulty getting a coherent statement from him this morning, even though he'd calmed down. Apparently he followed the same routine every night, though: first to his wife's for dinner, then to the bar, then back to the wife's, and finally home."

"As near as I know, he never deviated from

it. But I'm not home enough to be an authority on his comings and goings."

"Sharon, what about this peculiar living arrangement they had? Do you know anything about it?"

I held my beer bottle up and squinted at the sun through its bubbles. "Only what I told you last night."

"But what was the reason she threw him out? You don't discard a husband after all those years — he says they were married for forty — without some event to trigger it."

"All she would say was that she's been driven crazy long enough."

"How, though?"

"I don't know."

"Well, it's damned strange." He was silent a moment. "What about his job? He works for the Sunrise Blind Center."

"Yes. He leads one of the patients, a man named Sebastian, who restocks the grocery store racks with the brushes they make there."

"How'd he get into that?"

"Let's see." I considered. "The Center's been in that location — on Twenty-fourth Street, in the buildings that used to be Saint Luke's Catholic Church and Convent — for two or three years. Gus retired two years ago from his job as janitor at Edison School. Molly thought he needed something to keep him busy, and I think she asked if the Blind Center needed volunteers. They didn't, but they had this paying position, and they offered it to Gus."

Greg grimaced. "He's not a person I'd entrust my life to while crossing the street."

"Me either. Sometimes I think Sebastian should lead him instead of vice versa. All in all, he's a pretty poor murder suspect."

Greg began crumbling the edges of his sourdough roll. "He sure is, and I didn't get anything useful from the other tenants of your building. They are the strangest damned lot."

"Maybe I'm not around enough to notice it."

"The next time you are, take a good look. There's your manager, who evidently packs away beer on a round-the-clock schedule. There's the guy on the second floor who has a huge statue of a nude woman in his living room — and nothing else except the Murphy bed. And there's a woman on the third floor who looks exactly like a witch."

"Mrs. Neverman."

"Ah, you know her? She greeted me with a gun — the registration of which I've already verified — and refused to let me into her apartment because I might be a rapist. She thought nothing, however, of coming out into a dark hallway to talk to me."

"You, a rapist?"

"Yeah, you never can tell when I'll turn on you. Anyway, the Neverman woman claimed to be Antonio's best friend, but she couldn't tell me a single thing about her that shed any light on her death."

"She's probably suspicious of the police. She

certainly seems suspicious of everyone else, the way she creeps around there. I don't believe she's ever spoken to me."

"Huh." Greg pushed his blond hair off his forehead. "Finally, there's your corner grocer. Ye gods!"

"Mr. Moe? What did you think of him?"

"He's got to be totally crackers. Kept insisting Antonio had died because of some evil prophecy from her fortune teller, but he couldn't tell me who this prophetess of doom is or what she said."

"Oh, he gave you that too?" But Mr. Moe hadn't seemed to take the prophecy story seriously when I'd talked to him. Had he used it as a smokescreen? "What else did he say?"

"That she was in twice yesterday, once around five and again at seven. It fits with the time of death and the theory that she surprised her killer."

I nodded. But something about the timing disturbed me. What? "I suppose you ran a check on Mr. Moe?"

Greg took a swig of beer. "Makhlouf? Sure. Why?"

I shrugged. "He's one of these neighborhood characters that interests me."

"As well he should. His story is more interesting than most we hear."

"Tell me."

"Mr. Moe, as they call him, emigrated to New York from Saudi Arabia as a teenager. His father was reasonably well off, and he bought a grocery store in Brooklyn. After his death, Mr. Moe con-

40

tinued to operate it. He married, had one child."

"How'd he end up here?"

"The child, a daughter, married and moved here first. Then Mr. Moe's wife was killed by a mugger — for less than five dollars, all she had in her purse. Mr. Moe sold out and came here to be with his daughter."

"I never guessed that he had a family. He seems so solitary."

"He is, now. Tragedy followed him here. The daughter, her husband, and their baby died in that big apartment house fire on Church Street seven years ago. Mr. Moe lived with them, but he was out buying the paper when the blaze started. Several months later, he bought his current grocery store, probably to keep his mind off his loss."

I shook my head. "Symbolic, in a way."

"What is?"

"The name of the store: the Albatross. A man with all that tragedy hanging around his neck might choose it for just that reason."

Greg's dark-blond eyebrows pulled together. "I doubt he's all that literary-minded."

"His record's clean, though?"

"Reasonably. He's been hauled in on suspicion of discounting liquor in New York, and there was some indication he'd received stolen goods from time to time, but basically he's clean."

"So that's where your case stands."

"Yep. Unless you have something else to add."

"I don't."

"Too bad." Greg crumbled the remainder of his sourdough roll and tossed a piece to a pigeon that strutted nearby.

I glanced up at the ominous cloud of birds that suddenly descended on us. Seeing my frightened face, Greg put the bread down and spread empty hands to them. "Sorry. I forgot you're afraid of winged creatures."

"I know it's silly, but it's a common phobia. And phobias like that can kill you. I've read of people dying of shock from being exposed to perfectly innocent things they feared. So no more feeding the birds, okay?"

"Okay." He balled up the wrapper from his sandwich and stuffed it into the bag.

I started clearing the other picnic things, my eyes on the blanket. "Greg," I said, "about the murder weapon . . ."

"Yes?"

"What exactly was it?"

"A piece of drapery cord. Unfortunately, it was a type of common manufacture."

"It must have been cut off a longer piece, right?"

"Yes." A puzzled note crept into his voice.

"So, if you found the other piece, you could match them? By microscope?"

"We could. Why?"

"Just curious."

He watched me thoughtfully for a few seconds, then stood and folded the blanket. I retreated to the car as he tossed out a few remaining pieces of bread to the birds. We drove back to the Hall of Justice in silence.

When I had pulled up to the curb, I asked, "What do you think of Mr. Moe's fortune teller lead?"

"It's interesting. Why don't you follow up on it?"

"Okay. I've got some free time."

"Great." He got out of the car and leaned back in the window. "After all," he said with a grin, "I'd catch hell if I spent the taxpayers' money on an all-expense-paid trip to Fantasyland." He turned and loped off toward the Hall before I could reply.

Dammit! I thought as I watched him take the steps two at a time with his agile gait. Was the man ever serious?

5

By the time I had run some errands and found another parking space near my building, it was close to four o'clock. Anxious to check on Linnea, I hurried toward home, but was arrested by a familiar procession on the opposite sidewalk.

A small, gray man, stooped with arthritis, led a taller, heavyset man by the arm. The big man wore an Army surplus parka to which were attached dozens of brushes — hair brushes, wisk brooms, feather dusters, bottle brushes — each held in place by a wire hook. He carried several brooms. The little man lugged a worn cloth suitcase with bulging sides.

Gus and Sebastian, the brush man, going about business as usual less than twenty-four hours after Gus's wife's death. Or were they? What was the heavy-looking suitcase for?

The pair crossed the street toward me, Gus raising a hand in greeting.

"It's Miss McCone," he told Sebastian.

"Gus," I said, "I'm sorry about Molly."

He peered at me with red-rimmed eyes. The lines of his face and his jowls sagged dolefully. "Thanks, Miss McCone."

Sebastian shuffled forward and placed a hand on my arm.

"How're you?" I asked.

His face, scarred and pitted by the explosion that had blinded him, twisted. "Not good at all. This is a terrible day." To Gus, he added, "Why don't you go get the key from Tim? Miss McCone can help me upstairs."

Gus nodded and labored up the front steps with his suitcase.

I asked Sebastian, "How come you've got him working, with Molly dead less than a day?"

Sebastian adjusted the brooms under his arm. "We're not really working. I sent him in alone so I could tell you what's happened."

"What more could happen, after last night?"

"Plenty. And it's a damned shame!" His face flushed an angry red, the scars white against it. "This morning Gus had to give the cops a statement. They were pretty decent to him — even gave him a lift down there and back. But when they dropped him off at that sleazy joint he lives in, he found all his stuff stacked out on the porch."

"What?"

"Yeah. That bitch he rented from saw the story about Molly on the morning news. She said she was sorry for his trouble, but she couldn't have him there any more. Claimed Molly might've been offed by the Mafia and that they'd go for Gus next, so it wasn't safe having him in the house."

"Oh, for God's sake!"

"Yeah, all that bitch wanted was to rent the

room for more money. Gus has been there for so long, he wasn't paying near what it would fetch today. Sorry for his trouble, my ass!" He snorted.

"So what'd Gus do?"

"Came to me, at the Blind Center. What else could he do? He doesn't have any other friends."

"He must."

"Oh, sure, there're the fellows he plays dominoes with, but they're just first-name acquaintances. No, I'm all he has. It's a real shame when a person lives in a neighborhood for over forty years and doesn't have any friends and then gets kicked out of his room the day after his wife is killed. This sure is some town!" Sebastian took out a handkerchief and mopped his brow. "Makes me so mad I steam!

"Anyway," he went on, "we fed him lunch at the Center. Poor Gus can't even get himself a decent meal alone. Then Mr. Clemente — Herb Clemente, he's our director — called the cops and asked if it was okay for Gus to use Molly's apartment. They said fine, they were finished. A cop was there all morning, going through the place, but he was done by noon."

"So that's why the suitcase."

"Yeah. Gus left his other stuff at the Center. I said I'd come along and deliver some brushes on the way. It'd be a shame if he had to go back to that apartment all alone."

"You're a good friend to him."

"It's nothing. Gus has been mighty good to

me, and I couldn't do my work without him. What say we go in now? He's probably up there already."

I took his arm and we climbed to the second floor, Sebastian leaning heavily on me.

Gus stood on the blue rug where Molly's body had lain, the suitcase at his feet. When he saw Sebastian and me, he clasped his hands in a wringing gesture.

"Don't know what I'll do by myself." His voice was choked.

I let go of Sebastian and put my arm around Gus's narrow shoulders. "It's rough now, but things will get better."

He waggled his gray head helplessly. "I don't know how to do for myself. All those years, Molly took care of me. Even after she retired and threw me out, she took care of me."

"What did she do before she retired?" I knew very little of my dead neighbor's past.

"She was a clerk at Knudsen's." He named a Mission Street clothing store. "For thirty-five years, she stood behind a counter selling nylon stockings and underwear. Thirty-five years. And then she retired and threw me out. Said I'd driven her crazy long enough and that she deserved a little peace in her old age. But she still took care of me. I don't know what I'll do now."

I remembered the questions Greg had asked me. "Why did you drive her crazy, anyway?"

Gus's red-rimmed eyes became evasive. "How should I know? You know how women are."

47

Sebastian propped his brooms against the wall and felt for a chair. He lowered his bulky body onto it, sitting near the edge to avoid leaning on the brushes that hung from the back of his parka. "I tell you, Gus," he said, "something'll work out for you."

Again Gus shook his head. "Ain't nothing going to work out from now on. When the rent runs out on this place next month, where'll I go?"

"We'll find you some place to live," Sebastian said. "It's not as if you're poor. You've got your Social Security, and your wages from the Center, and there'll probably be some insurance money from Molly. All we've got to do is find you some place cheaper than this."

Gus looked far from convinced. To me he said, "What about Watney? I don't know nothing about taking care of cats."

I hesitated. I liked cats, but had never had one of my own. "If you want, I'll keep him."

"Would you?" A ripple of relief crossed Gus's drawn face. "Molly's got cat food and everything. You won't have to buy none for a long time." Eagerly, he went to the kitchen. "I'll pack it up right now."

"I seem to have acquired a pet," I said to Sebastian.

"No harm in that. Molly loved him. You will too."

"I guess. When did you last see . . . ." I paused, embarrassed. "I mean, talk to Molly?"

Sebastian smiled faintly. "Don't let it bother

48

you. Folks say stuff like that all the time. Seems handicaps make the folks who don't have them more uncomfortable than the folks who do. Anyway, it was late yesterday afternoon. Molly left a message with Mr. Moe for Gus to come by here before he took me home. She wanted him to fetch the clothes from the Laundromat — you know how folks will steal from the dryers over there. She was in your apartment when we came in, with your friend."

"Oh? What were they doing?"

"Just talking, I guess."

Gus came back, a cardboard carton clutched to his chest. "No, they weren't. Molly was reading her the riot act."

I felt a prickle of anxiety. "What about?"

He looked uncomfortable. "Probably her drinking."

"Ah," Sebastian said, "that's the one who drinks so much."

Was the whole world aware of it? "How did you know?"

"Molly told me. She found her lurching around in the trash bins last week."

"In the trash bins?"

"Yeah. She was taking — trying to take — the garbage out."

"Oh, God!" That was probably the day when, in a fit of manic housekeeping, Linnea had broken the handle of the toilet brush and incinerated an entire pot roast. "By the way, Sebastian," I said to cover my agitation, "do you happen to have

49

a toilet brush on you?"

He stood and felt over his right shoulder. I realized he could probably locate a given brush by touch faster than either Gus or I could by sight.

"Sorry," he said, "I'm fresh out." To Gus, he added, "Did you take those off of there?"

Gus looked hurt. "Why should I? The brushes are your department."

Sebastian grunted. "Could have swore I had them. We're selling out fast."

"Business is good, huh?" I asked.

"You bet. I've even added to my line. Shoelaces and rubber dishwashing gloves." He indicated the new items, tucked into his belt.

"They can't make those at the Blind Center."

"Nope. We get them wholesale. Sure you can't use a good shoelace?"

"None of my shoes need them. Would you drop a toilet brush off at my place when you get a chance?" I handed him the two dollars I knew it would cost.

"No trouble."

"And if I'm not there and Linnea acts strange, don't let it bother you." No sense in trying to hide the situation.

"She sure was upset yesterday," Gus commented. "Molly must've read her the riot act but good. I could tell, just from Molly's voice. Lord knows she read it to me often enough."

"What did she say to her?"

"Don't know. I just heard her through the open

door. She stopped when we came in and started talking about that sickly fern you've got. She talked on for a good five minutes before we could drag her away. Then I went to the Laundromat and Sebastian came up here to wait till I was done."

"How did Linnea act while Molly talked about the fern?"

"She was kind of snuffling and sulking, but she said goodbye pleasant."

"Hmmm." I was silent for a moment.

"You worried about your friend?" Gus asked.

"A little."

"You should be," he said sagely. "Next thing you know, she'll turn into another Tim O'Riley."

I suppressed a smile, comparing the petite Linnea to burly Tim, but, unfortunately, there was some truth in Gus's statement. And, even after years of steady beer-guzzling, Tim handled his alcohol far better than my friend.

Gus came forward with the cardboard carton. "Everything's in here except the litter box. It's got to be cleaned, so I'll bring it down later."

Good lord, I thought. A litter box. The poor cat had been cooped up since last night without one. I hoped Linnea had had the sense to . . . No, of course she hadn't. I'd be lucky if she hadn't thrown Watney out, thinking he'd wandered in by mistake. It was time I went down to check on both of them.

6

When I opened the apartment door, the cat leapt
out at me. He charged toward the little bed of
blue pebbles and plastic flowers that was the
owner's idea of lobby decoration and began to
root enthusiastically among the fake geraniums.
I smiled, remembering that Tim's pet peeve was
the inability among felines in the building to distinguish between this synthetic jungle and the out-
of-doors. Well, at least Watney had waited until
I got home.

I leaned against the door frame, suddenly tired
and looking forward to a cool glass of white wine.
The cat approached tentatively, glancing up at
me with wide yellow eyes before he sidled inside
and slithered down the hall. Apparently Watney,
with some reservations, had accepted his new
home.

I followed him, looking into the bathroom and
frowning at the wet, crumpled towels strewn on
the floor. Blond hair clogged the basin, and the
mirror was speckled. The main room was dark,
my new draperies drawn tightly across the bay
window. I jerked the cord, half expecting to find
Linnea curled up in the bed, but the light revealed
only twisted quilts. My friend must have taken

my advice to get out of here, and with good reason: Clothes were draped over every available piece of furniture, glasses stood on the shelves and table tops, ashtrays overflowed. Surely the place hadn't looked as bad this morning!

I sighed and went into the kitchen in quest of wine. Dirty dishes stood everywhere, some on the floor. I'd been busy the last few days and hadn't had time to wash them. But then, I hadn't been home long enough to dirty them either. I shoved aside a greasy frying pan and set down the carton of cat supplies, then opened the old electrified icebox that was built in to the wall and stared glumly into its depths. Besides every dish in the house, Linnea had used up all the wine.

"Jesus Christ," I said wearily. I shut the icebox and, after dishing out some food for the cat, went back to the main room. After a feeble attempt at straightening the disordered bedclothes, I picked up my purse and left.

I got as far as the front steps before I realized I didn't know where to go. There I sat, chin propped on my hand, watching the buses disgorge rush hour crowds at the corner stop. I should think, I told myself. I should think.

But what was there to think about? Linnea Carraway, my oldest friend, had turned into an obnoxious, self-centered bitch. And, in her post-divorce depression, she had veered so far off course that I could half-seriously entertain thoughts like those about the drapery cord. Not even my fondest memories of the days when we were growing up together in San Diego could change the fact of Linnea's drastic deterioration.

Still, the memories came rushing back as I sat here on the steps. Linnea was my friend from the days when we had asked the cards a question and, deep down, I still loved her.

Even now, my mind traveled to San Diego, to my bedroom in my parents' old, rambling house, to a younger Linnea sitting crosslegged on the floor as she dealt out a single game of solitaire. Her wheat-colored hair would be hitched up in horsetails on either side of her head, her pretty face pinched with concentration as she sat in the lamplight, her eyes pleading with the cards to make the game come out.

That was the trick: You asked the cards a question. If the game came out, the answer was "yes." If the cards stuck, the answer was "no." And the question, more often than not in those days, was: "Does he love me?"

Well, the "he" of Linnea's questions had loved her, for a while. He'd married her, given her two children, and left her for someone else, all in five short years. When the divorce was final, Linnea had left the kids at her mother's and come to me, her best friend, for sympathy and help in pulling the pieces of her life together. Dammit! How could I let her down?

Contrary to our younger days, I was now the strong one, the one who'd made the kind of life she wanted for herself. And Linnea: She had a broken marriage, two preschool kids parked with Grandma, and a full-blown nervous breakdown over the prospect of her spousal support running out in three years when, by the court's reckoning, she should have become self-supporting.

For weeks now I'd told her: "Look, three years is a fantastically long time. By then you could have gone to law school, or become an accountant. Hell, you could even have become a cop!"

But to Linnea, accustomed since her marriage to having her plans made for her, three years was all too short. She never disagreed with what I said, but she would sit there, staring at me as if I were speaking in tongues, and then reach for whatever liquor bottle was closest to hand. She went her sodden way, dropping her clothes on the floor, burning cigarette holes in the furniture, and in general playing havoc with my life. I couldn't understand what had happened to my gutsy, independent friend.

Linnea had always been a leader, one of those people who got things done with fanfare and flourish. In high school, she had hitchhiked to Los Angeles one weekend to see a rock star — and convinced him to come to San Diego for a benefit concert for our class's senior trip. She'd been the first in our crowd to backpack alone in the Sierras, to try skydiving, and to get a prescription for the Pill. While the rest of us went from school to dull jobs as secretaries or sales clerks or, in my case, security guards, Linnea wangled a job as a receptionist at a local TV station. In two years, she had become their first female news commentator. Her reportage, like her personal style, was decisive, forthright, and determined.

When Linnea met pro football player Jim Carraway, we all approved of the match. Jim was as strong and lively — a trifle domineering, though — as Linnea herself. The cards said "yes" about Jim, and Linnea married him.

And now, five years later, she had emerged from the marriage bedraggled, indecisive, and afraid of her own shadow. She searched the mirror for nonexistent wrinkles, talking of how she — at one hundred pounds — was "fatter and dumpier" than Jim's new woman. She complained of how her little girls loved their father more than her and would elect to live with him as soon as they reached the age when they could choose. She agonized about ever finding a job — who would hire anyone as "stupid" as her?

In the last three weeks, convinced there were no solutions to her problems, Linnea had begun to immerse herself in alcohol. Hours of drunkenness would alternate with periods of manic activity. She refused my help, refused professional help, and I didn't know what to offer next. So I let her walk all over me, feeling angry and guilty at the same time.

Well, I decided now, I wouldn't let her keep me from having my glass of wine. Why should I feel bad about bringing liquor home when she'd only buy it anyway? I got up and crossed to the Albatross Superette.

Mr. Moe was deep in conversation with a customer. The other man, a tall Latino with swooping black moustaches, glanced at me.

"Ah, Miss McCone," Mr. Moe said. "How are you tonight?"

"Fine, thanks."

"Have you met Mr. Clemente?" He nodded at his companion.

"I don't believe so."

"Mr. Herb Clemente is director of the Sunrise Blind Center. Miss Sharon McCone, from the building where the tragedy occurred, is a private detective."

"Pleased to meet you." The man called Clemente bowed in greeting. I half expected him to click his heels together.

"And I'm glad to meet you," I said. "In fact, I'd like to thank you for what you did for Gus Antonio."

He made a deprecating gesture. "*De nada.* The poor little man was completely helpless — more so than most of the residents of our Center. I merely made a phone call on his behalf." He paused, frowning. "Of course, something will have to be done about his future. That was only a temporary solution. Should you have any suggestions, Miss McCone, I'd be happy to hear them."

"If I think of anything, I'll let you know."

I went down the aisle to the refrigerated cases and picked out a bottle of Grey Riesling. On the way back, I checked out the freezer. Egg rolls, stuffed cabbage, TV dinners, cauliflower, artichoke hearts, lima beans . . . I stopped, looking down at them, then plucked out a package and carried it with the wine to the cash register.

On the curb outside, I checked my watch. It was close to six o'clock, but I was reluctant to go back to my dirty, depressing apartment. A few doors down the block were the welcoming lights of the neighborhood tavern, Ellen T's. I decided to stop off for a drink.

7

When I perched on the stool at the bar, Ellen T's skinny husband, Stanley, poured me a glass of the house white, my usual.

"How're you tonight?" he asked.

"Fair. You?"

"Surviving. Why'd you bring your own bottle along?" He gestured at the paper bag.

"I'm on my way back from a shopping trip, that's all. Do you think I could get a roast beef sandwich?"

Stanley frowned. "Is that going to be your dinner?"

"Guess so."

He shook his head. "Sharon, how many times have I told you that you've got to start eating better? You need fruit, green things. . . . By the way, the roast beef sandwich comes with a tossed salad this week, no extra charge."

I sighed. "Okay, Stanley, give me a salad too. But charge me for it, please."

I loved this bar. Big, motherly Ellen made the world's best sandwiches, and little Stanley dispensed sound, fatherly advice. Together they managed to preserve a bit of the fading tradition of the San Francisco neighborhood tavern.

While I ate, I looked around the room with the aid of the mirror over the bar. It was early, and there were only a couple of other people, men I didn't know, lined up on the stools. A woman who lived in my building was reading at one of the center tables, and a fellow I'd often seen in the nearby Laundromat sat in the front window bay, working out solitary moves on the chessboard.

I had finished my dinner and started on another glass of wine when a voice spoke over my shoulder. "Sharon McCone! We meet again so soon!"

I swiveled to face Herb Clemente. "Considering you live only a few blocks away, that's not surprising. You do live at the Center, don't you?"

"Yep. In what used to be the rectory. Makes me feel positively holy. How about having a drink with me?"

"I'd enjoy that." Picking up my wineglass and grocery bag, I followed him to a corner table. Stanley arrived shortly with Clemente's beer.

"Here's to new friends." Clemente raised his glass in a toast. "May they all be as pretty as you." He leaned forward, his elbows on the table, humor and keen intelligence lighting up his dark eyes.

"You flatter me," I said, "and I appreciate it."

"Good. Tell me, are you as clever as you are pretty?"

"I like to think I'm reasonably bright. Why?"

"Because if you are, maybe you can come up with an idea about what to do with Gus Antonio." He made a mock-sorrowful face. "I confess I've racked my brain with very few results."

"It's not an easy question." I considered. "Why not have him live at the Blind Center? Since he has to pick up and deliver Sebastian there every day, it might actually be more convenient."

Clemente sipped his beer. "That's a good idea, but unfortunately . . . it's impossible."

"Why?"

"We're funded by a combination of state and federal grants. One of their conditions is that no one but the director and certain designated staff members live on the premises with the residents — we prefer to call them that rather than patients. We have one 'illegal' right now — the handyman who also drives our truck. I couldn't risk another."

"Why is the handyman there?"

"He skipped out on his wife, a move I can fully sympathize with. She's a dreadful old woman. Anyway, he hasn't gotten it together to find another place, and I'd just as soon he didn't. It's useful to have him on the grounds. But try to tell that to the bureaucrats who approve our grants."

"Hmmm. That's too bad. It would be ideal for Gus."

"It would be more ideal if he could stay right where he is now. But he seems to think he can't

61

afford his dead wife's apartment."

"He's probably right. It's a one bedroom place; I have a studio, and even the rent for that is out of sight."

"Well, I wish we could think of something." Clemente set down his glass and signaled for another round. "Gus has done a damned good job helping Sebastian. He makes rounds with him every day but Sunday, and you could set your watch by him. I feel we should return the favor and help him now."

"Is it really necessary to restock those racks every day?" I asked. "Surely you don't sell that many brushes."

Stanley set our drinks down, and Clemente dug in his pocket for change. "With display racks, you have to keep on top of the situation. A poorly stocked rack looks like hell and doesn't attract customers."

"Ah, yes." I nodded. "I remember my days in the department store, folding and refolding layettes and baby blankets."

Clemente frowned. "You used to sell baby clothes?"

"Not for long. I was in the management training program of a San Diego store. They required three months of actual selling experience before you were funneled into your particular area of the operation. After the layettes, I went into security."

"So that's how you got into your line of work. You like it?"

"Department store security or private investigation?"

"Well, either."

"I hated the department store after a while. We had to snoop around pretending to be shoppers, with these big purses equipped with walkie-talkies. You can't imagine how sick you can get of looking through the same dresses every day. Anyway, when I'd saved enough money, I quit and went to college, at Berkeley. Afterwards, I joined one of the big detective agencies here in the city."

"Your degree prepared you for that?"

"No. It was in sociology, and it made me damned near unemployable. My security background got me the job."

"And you're with that firm now?"

"Not now. We had . . . a disagreement a few years ago. I'm not very responsive to authority. All Souls Legal Cooperative is where I work. But here I am, telling you my life story. What about you — how'd you get into the brush business?"

Clemente grinned broadly. "I'm a psychology graduate, and I've been a government parasite my whole career. I started as a prison guard while attending college. In the fifteen years since then, I've operated a halfway house and directed programs for counseling parolees. When the job with the Blind Center came up, I jumped at the chance to get away from felons."

"I can understand. I don't deal with too many, but a lot of the characters I come across are pretty

63

shady. . . ." My attention was drawn to the door behind Clemente, where Linnea stood. "Oh, there's my friend." I motioned for her to come over.

Linnea waved and walked toward the table. She wore jeans and a suede jacket that hugged her trim little figure. Her wheat-colored hair hung free, framing her face, which was still tanned from the Southern California sun she worshiped.

I made the introductions, and Linnea joined us, ordering a stinger in response to Clemente's offer of a drink. "Hey, this is great," she said to me. "You weren't at the apartment when I got back from shopping, so I went over to the Superette, and Mr. Moe said he'd seen you go in here. Not bad detective work for an amateur, huh?"

"Damned good." Linnea was sober and definitely in her manic stage. She smiled brightly and made animated gestures while she spoke, the many rings on her fingers flashing.

Clemente sat up straighter, looking at her with visible interest.

"Well, I've studied detection with one of the best," Linnea replied, grinning warmly at me, our hot words on the telephone forgotten.

"So you went shopping?" I asked.

"For food and cleaning stuff. I had to. The place is a pit." To Clemente, she added, "I'm staying with Sharon, and I've managed to destroy her apartment. Why I'm such a slob. . . ." She smiled helplessly.

Clemente smiled back, obviously enchanted.

I studied them thoughtfully. A new romantic interest might be just what Linnea needed.

"Ah," Clemente said, "you're staying over there." He jerked his head in the direction of my building. "Did you know the woman who was murdered?"

Linnea nodded, her eyes wide. "Did you?"

"Oh, yes. Her husband works for the Blind Center. In fact, it was Mrs. Antonio who suggested he apply to us."

"How did that come about?" I asked.

"Gus had retired and was picking up bad habits. What they were, she wouldn't say, but she wanted something for him to do so he would stay out of trouble. All she had in mind was a volunteer position, but fortunately we were able to pay him a small — very small — salary."

Linnea leaned her chin on her hand, affecting fascination. Clemente's gaze slid back to her.

"Even though you're only an amateur detective, do you have any suspicions about who killed her?" he asked.

She shook her head. "It's strange, coming right after she'd had such a bad session with her spiritual advisor."

"Spiritual advisor?" Clemente and I chorused.

"Oh, that's what she called her fortune teller. She said Madame Anya hadn't been able to give her any advice that wouldn't lead her into a worse predicament than she was already in."

"What kind of predicament?" I asked.

"She wouldn't say, but she was very upset. She said it was all because of the cards."

"Good grief. Who is this Madame Anya?"

Linnea looked surprised. "Don't you know?"

"No. I've never heard of her."

"But she lives in your building."

"A fortune teller in the building? That's a new one!"

"She's been there a long time. I guess you're not around enough to meet the other tenants." Linnea's reproachful look indicated that I wasn't around enough to suit her, either. "Anyway, it's Mrs. Neverman, on the third floor."

"Mrs. Neverman is Madame Anya?" I thought of the hatchet-faced woman, whom Greg had described as a witch.

"Yes. Wait, I'll show you." Linnea rummaged in the bottom of her big canvas purse.

I glanced at Clemente. He wore an amused smile.

"Here it is!" Linnea extended a tattered handbill to me. It was crudely printed, with Tarot figures around its edges. I took it and read aloud:

" 'Madame Anya — All Welcome.' " I looked up at Linnea. "Is this serious?"

"Keep going," she said. "You won't believe it."

The handbill was headlined: CARD READER — PSYCHIC READER — SPIRITUAL ADVISOR. I read on, into the fine print.

One visit will convince you! Madame Anya

has the God-given Power to Heal by Prayer. What you see with your eyes, your heart will believe. Are you suffering? Are you sick? Do you need help? Do you have bad luck? Bring your problems to Madame Anya today and be rid of them tomorrow. She advises on all affairs of life. There is no problem too great she can't solve. She calls your friends and enemies by name without asking you a single word and reunites the separated. Madame Anya has devoted a lifetime to this work. From the four corners of the world they have come to her, men and women of all races and walks of life. Guaranteed to remove evil influence and bad luck. Lifts you out of sorrow and darkness and starts you on the way to success and happiness. Madame Anya invites you to her home. What your eyes see, your heart will believe!

It ended by promising a free lucky charm to all comers, and stated that all readings were private and confidential.

"Good Lord!" I exclaimed. "Just look what I've been missing. She certainly didn't bring Molly good luck, though."

"Or me," Linnea said. "Would you look at this stupid charm?" She held up a little plastic statue of a bluebird dangling from a key chain. "Did you ever see the likes of it? No wonder she gives them out free!"

I looked at her curiously. "You went to her?"

"Once. Molly thought she could help me. And I . . ." She faltered. "I was ready to try anything." Her chin came up defiantly.

Clemente looked perplexed.

"What was it like?" I asked.

"Strange."

"Did she tell you anything useful?"

"No," she replied sulkily. "If you're so interested, why don't you go see her yourself?"

"I think I'll do that," I said, standing. "In fact, I'll do it right now."

Linnea looked up in surprise. "My hard-headed, practical friend is going to visit a fortune teller?"

"Why not?"

She grinned. "Why not? We can compare notes later."

I thanked Clemente for the drink, and he told me to stop in at the Blind Center sometime for a tour. At the bar, I paused to remove the lima beans from my grocery bag. The package was slightly damp, but still firm. I slipped it into my purse and checked the wine with Stanley for safe-keeping. Linnea was starting in on her second stinger; by the time she got home, she'd be ready to drink all night, and I didn't want the wine there to tempt her.

As I went out the door, I glanced back at the table. Linnea and Clemente were laughing, their heads close together. Her knee was pressed firmly against his thigh.

8

The dim orange bulb on the third-floor landing did little to illuminate the hall. I waited as heavy footsteps approached from within Mrs. Neverman's apartment. The door opened a few inches, and I stared down the long barrel of a .22 revolver. Mrs. Neverman's face peered out over the security chain, curiosity and apprehension accentuating the forward thrust of her jaw.

"Yes? What do you want?" Her voice grated harshly.

"Mrs. Neverman? I'm Sharon McCone, from the first floor."

"Yes?"

"You're the person who advertises herself as Madame Anya?"

"I am." Proudly, she drew herself up to her full height.

"My friend, Linnea Carraway, came to you for a . . . a consultation." I was beginning to feel silly, so I plunged ahead. "I was also a friend of Molly Antonio."

"Do you wish a consultation?" she asked impatiently.

"Uh, yes, I do." I had to get inside somehow.

"Then come in, please."

Unhooking the chain, she slipped the gun into a table drawer and ushered me into a small, dark room crammed with heavy furniture. In spite of its dimness, it must have received good sun during the day because African violets bloomed everywhere: on tables and shelves, even on the floor. A big, old-fashioned buffet was banked like an altar with plants and dozens of candles shaped like birds. I stared at them, fascinated.

Mrs. Neverman turned to me. "Please sit down."

I looked for a chair, but heard a sudden flapping sound. I jerked my head up. A great blur of black feathers dove at me.

Crying out, I covered my head with my arms. "My God, get it out of here!"

Mrs. Neverman looked startled, but held out her arm. The creature flew over and perched on her wrist. It was a crow, with a wingspread of at least two feet.

"Goodness, honey," the fortune teller said, "don't let Hugo frighten you!"

My heart beat fast, and my palms felt clammy but I sat down and attempted to act calm. "Sorry — it's a silly fear I have. He's awfully large, isn't he?"

She regarded the bird fondly. "Not really. He's a fish crow. They're native to the Gulf states, and much smaller than the standard American crow. They're just as easily trained, though. I've taught Hugo to say a few words." She took the bird to an ornate cage and deposited it within. I relaxed somewhat.

Mrs. Neverman seated herself in an armchair opposite me. In spite of her earlier attempt at proud bearing, her shoulders now hunched defensively under her maroon velvet robe. She seemed painfully aware of her ugliness, and the knowledge took a toll that showed in her every movement.

Calmly, she said, "Our friend's death, honey — I prophesied it."

"You mean you told her that she would be murdered?" I couldn't keep the horror out of my voice.

"No. I would never go that far."

"What did you tell her, then?"

"I can't say. My readings must be kept confidential. But it was all there — a terrible aura."

The fortune teller was using Molly's death for advertising purposes. I frowned.

"Now, what's your problem, honey?" she asked.

"Problem?"

"You came to me. You must have a problem."

"I . . . uh . . ."

"I see, honey. You don't want to talk about it to a stranger. But that's all right, that's all right. Why don't I give you the standard reading. Then you'll feel more free."

And maybe by then I could invent a problem. "All right, Mrs. Neverman."

"You just call me Anya, honey. This is your

71

first reading I bet."

"Yes."

"Well, you just relax. Do you have something with you that has special significance? Some jewelry? A keepsake, maybe?"

I looked down at my folded hands, where my mother's signet ring circled my left middle finger. She had given it to me when I turned twenty-two, explaining it always passed down to the oldest daughter. One of my few superstitions was the luck I believed it brought me.

Anya's eyes followed mine. "May I see it a minute?"

Reluctantly I pulled it off and dropped it into her outstretched palm, feeling a little lost without it. Her large fingers curled, and she bent her head to examine it. In the silence that followed, a growing tension gripped me. I realized I was afraid of what she might say and, even more, that I would believe it.

"It's a very old ring," Anya finally said. "A family heirloom."

"Yes." One didn't need ESP to guess that.

"The ring is a European type, so your heritage can't be all Indian."

"As a matter of fact, I'm only an eighth Indian. Everybody else in my family looks Scotch-Irish except me, I'm what they call a 'throwback' — and believe me, I took plenty of ribbing about it when I was growing up."

Anya's dark eyes watched me intently. "I see. You were a very loved child, you know. The ring was a gift from your mother."

Again, it was a guess, since it was a woman's ring. Anya didn't have mystical powers, but her mind operated logically. She might have made a good detective.

"The ring," she went on, "always passes down to the oldest daughter."

I started. Just another guess, I reminded myself.

"You believe this ring has powers." She looked shrewdly at me. "Luck, maybe?"

"Maybe." I sat up straighter.

"Yes, honey, you're not a person who likes to admit she's superstitious. The ring really does have powers, but they're not strong enough. Not nearly strong enough for the trouble that lies before you."

"Trouble?" A spurt of irrational anxiety shot through me.

"Yes, trouble, honey. There's trouble in your home."

I relaxed. After all, Linnea had been to see her. Naturally she knew all about it.

"Your friend has many problems, the one who's staying with you. She makes them worse with drink. Oh, I tried to warn her. I told her she must pray to be cured of this sickness and work for the strength to overcome her difficulties."

"What did she say?"

"Your friend does not accept advice easily."

That accounted for Linnea's sulky behavior when I'd asked her what the fortune teller had said. "No, she doesn't."

"You know, your friend has made a shambles of your home. But this is only the beginning. She will get worse, honey, much worse. You will need great strength to get through it." Anya paused and pointed dramatically at me. "In the next week you will struggle hard against the death of friendship. There is a dark-haired man who speaks falsely to you. Do you know who I mean? There is a light-haired man who you think is your friend. Watch out for him; he's capable of betraying you. There are dangers in believing what anyone says. You must be on guard of lies and try to recognize them when they're spoken."

Involuntarily, I shivered. I didn't believe a word of it, but, like a soap opera, Anya's acting had the power to suck me in against all my better intentions.

The fortune teller extended my ring to me. "Yes, honey, this is not strong enough to protect you from these troubles. But I can help you, if you let me."

I slipped the ring back on my finger. "How?"

"I will pray for you. Do you see those candles?" She motioned at the birds on the buffet.

"Yes."

"They're special candles — natural wax, only the purest ingredients. And they're shaped like birds, so my prayers will fly up to God. Every night at midnight for an entire week, I will light one of them for you and pray. I guarantee your troubles will vanish."

It was an interesting sales pitch. "How much

do the candles cost?"

"Oh, honey." She waved a dismissing hand. "Not much for you. Only five dollars apiece. Surely that isn't too much to protect yourself from this evil?"

Thirty-five dollars, plus whatever this reading cost. And she wouldn't even be out the price of the candles, since it was doubtful I would show up at midnight, demanding to watch her burn them.

I glanced at the candles again, feigning interest. "I don't know. I don't get paid until Friday."

"But surely then you'll want me to pray for you."

Anya apparently didn't extend credit — even with such dire evil hovering on the horizon. "Probably I will. I'll let you know."

Suspiciously she asked, "You do have the five dollars for the reading?"

"Of course."

She extended a greedy hand for the bill, and when she had received it, gave me a lucky charm like the one Linnea had. "I guarantee my prayers will save you much pain, honey. I suggested I pray for your friend, but she said she would rather spend the money on liquor. She was very rude."

"I'm sorry about that. Did you light candles often for Molly?"

"Oh, honey, I did. I planned to this last time, even though there seemed little hope of saving her."

"Hmmm. Did you hear what happened to Gus?"

"Besides losing Molly, you mean?"

"Yes." I explained what Sebastian had told me.

"Poor little man." Anya shook her head. "Where will he go now?"

"Temporarily he can stay at Molly's. But after the first of the month no one knows. I was talking to Herb Clemente earlier . . ."

"Clemente!" Anya's eyes narrowed.

"Yes. He's director of the Sunrise Blind Center."

"I know who he is!"

"What's the matter?"

"You're not a friend of that swine?"

"I just met him tonight. What's wrong?"

"Wrong? I'll tell you what's wrong! Look around this place. Do you see anyone?" She waved her arm violently.

I looked. "Just the bird."

"That's right." She bobbed her head emphatically. "Just little Hugo and me. Jeffrey Neverman isn't here and hasn't been since that swine talked him into leaving home."

"Wait a minute, Anya. Who's Jeffrey? Your son?"

"My son?" Her voice rose an octave. "Jeffrey Neverman is my husband. At least he was until that Clemente lured him away from here."

I remembered Clemente's handyman, who had left his "dreadful old" wife. No wonder Clemente had smiled when Linnea mentioned Anya.

"How did Clemente lure him away?" I asked.

"By any number of vicious lies. That swine has an evil aura. He probably convinced Jeffrey he should run after younger, prettier women. Just because I'm ten years older than him is no reason to lust after young flesh." Anya's hand went to her face, and she rubbed it like a painful bruise.

I looked away from her anguish.

"He can't have much luck with the ladies, though," she muttered, more to herself than to me. "How could he, sleeping on the floor in the basement of that old church?"

"He lives in the old church at the Blind Center?"

She nodded. "And, after all he's done, you must think I'm a fool to worry about him. But it's damp and drafty there, and he catches cold so easily. Why he chooses to stay . . ." She paused, eyes swimming. "Yeah, I still love him. Dumb, isn't it?"

"Not really," I said, feeling uncomfortable in my new role of confidante.

"Well, I do, honey. I do." She sighed heavily and blew her nose on a lace-bordered handkerchief.

I asked, "How did Jeffrey get his job at the Center?"

She sniffed disdainfully. "I don't know as you can call it a job. He never does a lick of real work. Jeffrey met Herb Clemente when he got out of prison. Clemente gave him some counseling, but it didn't take. Jeffrey still didn't have

77

a job when Clemente and the Blind Center moved in over there on Twenty-fourth Street, so he looked Clemente up. Clemente let him run some errands. Then, two months ago, Jeffrey up and informed me he was leaving, to go live there in the church."

"Why was he in prison?"

Her long jaw became set. "Jeffrey used to be a trucker. He made good money, was even going to start his own company. But, no, he couldn't be satisfied with that. He stole stuff from the loads he hauled, and they caught him. He went to prison for two years, and I stood by him the whole time. A lot of good it did me — look at the reward I got!"

I didn't know what to say. "I'm sorry."

"Oh, honey, that's life. That's life." She rose heavily. "But it won't go on much longer. I'm going to get him back soon. I have a plan. You just wait and see if I don't get him back." She held the door open for me. "You let me know about those candles on Friday, all right?"

I said I would and started downstairs.

On the dim third-floor landing, I remembered the lima beans in my purse. The package was wet and soggy, in spite of whatever insulation my thin macrame bag provided. I looked at my watch: nine-thirty, only three and a half hours since I had bought them. I hurried downstairs and outside.

The windows of the Albatross Superette were dark. Mr. Moe must have closed up early. I peered at the second story, where the grocer lived. No light showed there either.

My momentum fizzled out, and I stood still. What to do now? The night was relatively young.

Well, Mr. Moe wasn't available, but maybe Sebastian could use some company. Even though the brush man was blind, I suspected he knew more of what went on in the neighborhood than those of us who could see. I dumped the soggy lima beans in a waste receptacle and started off for Twenty-fourth Street.

9

Even at nine-thirty, Twenty-fourth Street was well populated. People wandered along the sidewalks, in and out of the bars and hole-in-the-wall cafes. I walked along more purposefully.

The Sunrise Blind Center sat back from the sidewalk in shadow, its grounds surrounded by an iron fence. I was about to cross the street toward it when two figures came through the gate. Clemente and Linnea. They turned onto the sidewalk, walking close together, Clemente's arm draped across Linnea's shoulders. The Center's director was a fast worker. For that matter, so was my friend.

I watched them walk away, then crossed and pushed through the creaking gate. A cement path led toward the floodlit front of the old church. All was quiet.

The church was adobe, its dark-timbered roof meeting in a peak over the front entry. The cross that had once adorned the peak was gone, and a brilliantly-hued, primitive mural of a sunrise spread across the triangular space below the roofline. Above the door, a crudely lettered inscription read:

"Sunrise, Beginning of New Life and Hope."

Odd, for a blind center, I thought. None of the patients — or residents, as Clemente preferred to call them — would be able to see it.

The cement path continued around the building. There were lights in the former rectory and the convent, set far back on the deep lot. Another light spread across the path from a ground-level window of the church. On impulse, I pounded on a side door.

A tall, slender man with gray-flecked hair and a scraggly moustache answered. I recognized him as someone I'd seen around my apartment building. He stood in the doorway, swaying slightly, his pupils dilated as if he were high on something. His eyes focused on me, and he drew his bushy brows together in a laborious frown.

He said, "I didn't order any pizza."

"That's good, because I didn't bring any."

The frown stayed in place. "Maybe not so good. Now that I think of it, I could use a pizza. Can't remember when I ate last." He pondered for a moment. "No, I really can't remember. What do you want?"

"Are you Jeffrey Neverman?"

"Yes." His tone was dubious, as if he weren't really sure. "Who are you?"

"Sharon McCone. I live in Anya's building."

"Anya. Anya of the face like a foot." Neverman swayed into the door frame, then recovered himself. "But I shouldn't speak of Anya that way. She *is* my wedded wife. Come in."

I stepped inside and almost toppled down a

flight of stone steps. Neverman's hand caught my shoulder. I felt its cold through my sweater.

"Careful there," he said. "We have to go down to the basement."

Clutching the railing, I followed him. It would have been highly appropriate had he held a candle aloft rather than the flashlight he flicked on. He led me down a narrow hallway with overhead pipes and heating ducts to a small room.

A sleeping bag lay on an air mattress in its center. Next to it stood a low wooden crate which held a portable radio, a pile of books, and an ashtray filled with what looked like marijuana roaches. The candle I'd envisioned flickered atop a wine bottle on the floor. The room reeked of grass.

"Please have a seat," Neverman said. "You take the couch." He giggled shrilly.

I dropped onto the sleeping bag, and my host sat crosslegged on the floor. He reached for one of the roaches in the ashtray, lit it, and offered it to me.

I shook my head. "No, thanks. I've got to keep straight tonight."

He grimaced. "You *must* be a friend of Anya's. She's always straight. If that broad could ever get laid back . . . so what's happening with her, anyway?"

"Her friend, Molly Antonio, got murdered."

"I heard."

"Anya says she prophesied it."

"Shit! She can't even lose a friend without

claiming she saw it all with her precious pow-ers!"

"I take it you don't believe in them."

Neverman glanced at the roach, which had gone out, and regretfully placed it in the ashtray. "Of course I don't. I lived with that woman for five years, off and on. It's nothing but a bunch of convoluted crap!" He looked at me slyly and added, "You don't have any dope on you, by any chance?"

It wasn't a commodity I normally carried. "Sorry, no."

"I figured not. A friend of that broad's wouldn't."

"I'm not really a friend of hers," I said quickly. "But from what I do know of her, I'm surprised she's married to somebody like you. Isn't she a lot older?"

"Fifteen years. I'm forty, she's fifty-five, but she likes to claim it's only ten."

"How come you married her, anyway?"

He shrugged. "Money. She had some, and I had a use for it."

"I didn't think fortune tellers made that much."

"They don't. Anya's got a little inheritance squirreled away. I thought if I married her, I'd get the use of it. But that broad is as tightfisted as they come."

"What were you going to use it for?"

"My business. I was going to start my own trucking line. 'Neverman's Intercoastal Truck-ing,' it would of been called. I'd have gotten rich by now if she'd let me have the money."

"It's a good business to get rich in."

"You can say that again!" Neverman's face contorted with sudden anger, and he struck his fist against his thigh. "Damn that stupid broad! She's saving the money for a rainy day, she says. So I end up here, living like some goddamned hippie, instead of owning my own company. That'll all change soon. It'd better!"

"Exactly how did you end up here?" I asked.

His glance was veiled. "Anya didn't tell you?"

"No," I lied.

"Let's just say I made some bad moves, then. I don't want to talk about it. One thing I will tell you, it's a hell of a lot better living like this than with her and her wax birds and that goddamn crow. I put up with it for over two years this last stretch, and then I couldn't take it any more. Even prison was better."

"Prison?"

"Figure of speech." His eyes shifted away from mine.

"So what do you do here?"

"Handyman work. Drive the truck. Anything they need me for. You see the mural over the front door?"

"Yes."

"Mine." Momentarily, he looked pleased. "That was one of the things I liked doing. You should see the job I've got upstairs, though. That's going to be a bitch."

"Why?"

"Because of the fire they had, the roof's burned out. I've got to put on a new one, or the Feds won't renew one of our grants."

Dimly, I recalled that St. Luke's had sold out to the Blind Center after fire had destroyed part of the nave. It surprised me that it hadn't been fixed long ago. To escape this oppressive little room, I asked, "Could I take a look?"

"Sure. Why not?" He rose, extending his hand to help me. In the candlelight, he looked less faded and down-and-out. I could understand how he would hold a certain scruffy charm for a woman like Anya.

The air in the upstairs vestibule was damp, the gloom as deep as in Neverman's room. He groped along the wall and flipped on a light. I went into the main part of the church.

In the shadows, I made out the crouching shapes of the pews. Stained-glass windows glowed at the sides. Toward the front, where the altar presumably had been, I saw only darkness.

I went down the aisle. Neverman's footsteps echoed behind me. Startled by a sudden rush of chill air, I stopped. Neverman's body nudged mine. I looked up at the roof, but saw only stars and wispy, low-lying clouds.

"That's where the roof's burned out." Neverman's breath tickled my ear.

I stepped away from him. "Isn't there a light in here?"

"Only over the altar. The fire wrecked the rest of the wiring." He turned his flashlight on the

85

ruined roof, shining it along the charred and jagged beams.

"Why hasn't it been fixed before?" I asked. "The Center's been in here a long time."

He shrugged. "Government grants don't give you that kind of money. Now Herb's got the bright idea of having me do the work. That'll be a trip."

The darkness was making me edgy. "Why don't you turn on that light so I can get a look at the altar?"

"What do you need a light for?" He turned the flash on my face, and I blinked and stumbled back against the first pew.

Neverman set the flash down and took hold of both of my arms, forcing me to sit. In the upward rays of the flashlight, his lean face looked like a bemoustached skull. He knelt in front of me.

"Hey, you know," he said softly, "you're really a pretty lady."

Unlike Clemente's flattery, Neverman's words chilled me.

Letting go of one arm, he pushed up the sleeve of my sweater and began stroking me with his fingers. His nails were long and rasped on my skin.

"Cut it out, Jeffrey," I said firmly.

"Aw, pretty lady, how about it? You and me, we could really get it on."

I removed his hand and pulled down my sleeve. "I don't think so."

He snorted and stood up. "You may not be Anya's friend, but you two would make a good pair."

Relieved that my calm response had worked, I stood up too. "Now how about letting me see the altar?"

He shrugged angrily and strode up the aisle. In a moment pale light came up on the raised platform. It increased in intensity until it shone bright as daylight.

"It's a dimmer switch," Neverman called. "They probably used it to make the services more dramatic. Can't you see Anya with one of these? She could use it like this."

The light on the altar paled again.

"Your life up to this time has been happy, honey," he mimicked in a harsh voice that sounded remarkably like the fortune teller's. "But . . ."

The light increased several shades.

"I see great trouble ahead. This trouble, it is awful."

Still brighter.

"Honey, I can't begin to describe this awful trouble. But . . ."

The light flashed to full intensity.

"There is help ahead! I will pray for you, honey! And rip you off with my wax birds!"

It would have been funny, had his anger not been so fierce. I went up the aisle and joined him next to the round light switch in the vestibule.

"You didn't like my little performance," he said mockingly.

"Not particularly. I . . ."

The front door opened behind us. Sebastian entered, tapping along with a white cane.

"Neverman? Is that you in here?"

"Christ!" Neverman muttered. "He's like something out of Charles Addams."

Sebastian could not have missed the comment, but he merely said, "Who's with you?"

"It's only me, Sebastian," I said. "Sharon McCone."

"Miss McCone! You do turn up in the most amazing places."

"So what do you want, Sebastian?" Neverman asked impatiently.

"You've got a phone call up at the dormitory."

"Oh, yeah? From who?"

"It sounds like your wife."

"Jesus Christ!" He twisted the light switch angrily, and the church subsided into darkness. Without another word, he stomped out the door.

"The man has a dreadful temper," Sebastian commented.

"I guess. Shall I help you back to the convent . . . dormitory, I mean?"

Sebastian's scarred face contorted into a smile. "That's not necessary. I get around perfectly well with my cane in places I'm familiar with."

I glanced at my watch. It was close to eleven, and I was in no mood for further conversation. "In that case, I'll be going. Maybe I'll see you tomorrow at Gus's new apartment?"

"Very likely, Miss McCone."

Sebastian left me on the path in front of the church, where the full moon looked down coldly through the twisted branches of a tree. Yawning, I decided to go home for some sleep. I'd talk with Mr. Moe, the dark-haired man who spoke falsely to me, in the sane light of morning.

10

The sane light of morning saw me called back to All Souls for a pretrial conference on the redwood hot tub case. It had not been a particularly dramatic investigation, but I'd discovered that the so-called contractor had used substandard materials. We had, as Hank put it, an airtight case against an outfit whose tubs did not hold water.

By one o'clock I was officially on vacation again. I returned to my office to fetch my bag and check for messages. There were two: one from Greg and one from Linnea.

Greg's message simply said, "What's new?" Briefly, I wondered if this indicated repentance over the sarcastic tone on which he'd departed yesterday. No, I concluded, it probably meant he was bored and hoped I'd take him to lunch. I discarded the note in the wastebasket.

The second message was disconcerting. Linnea asked that I call her; it was urgent. I lined the slip up on the blotter and stared thoughtfully at it, tapping my fingers on the edge of the desk. My friend had taken a turn for the better, but now I wasn't sure how long it had lasted.

When I'd arrived home the night before, all

had been quiet in the apartment. A cloud of warm, steamy air and the scent of Linnea's favorite perfume greeted me as I entered.

Things must be picking up, I thought. She's taken a shower.

I went into the bathroom and flicked on the light. The mirror was polished, the basin scoured clean. Fresh towels hung on the racks, the old ones dumped into the wicker hamper. A note, Scotch-taped to the mirror, said:

"Sharon — Sorry about the mess. I'll try to do better. Love, L."

I looked beyond the note to my face, which wore an expression of shame. Linnea meant well. I didn't give her enough credit for trying.

I felt my way down the hall to the main room, where a night light burned. It revealed Linnea's sleeping form in the bag on the floor, the cat curled up beside her. The room was orderly, and a Ghirardelli chocolate bar was propped against a vase of fresh daffodils on the coffee table. My stomach knocked as I thought of Greg.

Calm down, I told myself. So what if he was here? So what if he discovered Linnea was staying with me and talked to her? There's nothing suspicious about the fact I haven't mentioned her to him; we haven't been seeing one another since she arrived.

But I still felt uncomfortable and knew it was directly linked to that missing piece of drapery cord.

I undressed, sniffing appreciatively at the clean,

scented sheets as I slipped into bed and pulled the heavy quilts over me. I should get my mind off that elusive piece of cord and concentrate on the facts of the murder.

Try motive, Sharon.

What motive could Linnea possibly have? She liked Molly. So they quarreled. So Molly bawled her out about her drinking. You don't strangle a person over something like that.

Not if you're rational.

Is Linnea?

Of course she is.

Is she?

Well, maybe not all the time. But look at the other facts: Molly's apartment was searched. And she was preoccupied — worried, really — about something the day of her death. That alone should tell you her murder was well motivated. Maybe even well planned.

Why don't you get off Linnea and look for the real killer? When you find him, you'll know your friend is innocent.

Give it a try, huh?

My next impression was the smell of freshly brewed coffee. I struggled up on one elbow as Linnea emerged from the kitchen, wearing a yellow terrycloth caftan, her wheat-colored hair in childish braids. She looked at me with the expression of a naughty six-year-old.

"Are you mad at me?"

I could remember her asking the same thing in exactly the same way when she'd knocked me into the creek at the Girl Scout picnic. "Not now. Thanks for the coffee." I made space for it on the bedside table.

"You're welcome." She sat down crosslegged on the bed. Her fresh-scrubbed face was cheerful, and her lips curled up contentedly. "I tried to clean the place up last night, and I promise I'll finish the job today."

"You must have really dervished around here," I said, recalling how she and Clemente had left the Blind Center after nine-thirty.

Linnea chuckled. The verb "to dervish" was one of our old terms, part of that private language that springs up between close friends. "You should have seen me. It was sort of like doing penance."

"Penance was easier than cleaning house." I remembered the comforting shape of the rosary beads as I knelt in the shadows of Holy Name back home, then shook off the thought. I'd quit going to church many years ago. "So what do you have planned for today?"

"I thought I'd go to the Laundromat and do some ironing. Maybe I'll bake us some bread. I want to be home in case . . ." She flushed prettily.

"In case Herb calls?"

She nodded, her eyes alight. "Sharon, he took me up to the Blind Center last night. You should see his place!"

"He lives in what used to be the rectory, right?"

"Yes. It's beautiful — all parquet floors and

dark wood and adobe. He's got these handwoven Mexican rugs on the walls, and pottery and statues that look pre-Columbian, and a waterbed that I'm looking forward to . . ." She paused, both embarrassed and pleased.

I grinned, and she grinned back, and then we both snickered like boys in the locker room.

"Just what the doctor ordered," Linnea said.

"It's amazing what a new man will do for your spirits." I got up and went to the closet. "Anyone who can make you turn to housework . . ." I gestured at the chocolate bar on the coffee table. "Did you buy the candy too?"

"Yesterday afternoon, at Safeway. I ate the last one that cop gave you, and I wanted to replace it."

With a flash of relief, I took out a black wool pantsuit and reached for the clothes brush. "Lord, you didn't have to do that!" And I wished she hadn't; the chocolate bar she had eaten had been Hershey's, an excellent brand. As far as serious chocolate lovers were concerned, the best thing about Ghirardelli was the wrapper.

"Linnea," I said, brushing at my jacket, "Gus told me Molly was here with you around five o'clock the day she was killed. How did she seem?"

Linnea frowned and began fiddling with one of her braids. "What do you mean?"

"Was she happy? Unhappy? Upset about the fortune teller?"

"Oh." She considered. "I'd say she wasn't in

94

the best of moods."

"How so?"

"Well, she . . . she was kind of short-tempered."

"About what?"

She shrugged sullenly. "I don't really remember."

I tried another tack. "Was that when she mentioned her bad session with Madame Anya?"

"Yes. Did you go see her last night?"

"Uh-huh. She's a strange lady."

"Old bat!"

"She's not that bad. She's lonely."

Again a sullen shrug.

"Anyway," I said, "Madame Anya wouldn't tell me about the session with Molly — she claims it has to remain confidential. What exactly did Molly tell you?"

Linnea pressed a hand to her forehead. "Wow, everything kind of blends together lately."

"Since you've been drinking so much."

Instantly, I regretted it. Linnea lowered her eyes to her lap and picked at a thread on her caftan. In a moment, she said, "Why do you have to harp on that today? Why is it that every time we talk you have to bring that up?"

I wasn't aware I had been. "I'm sorry. You meant, things are mixed up since your divorce and all."

"Yes, since my divorce and all." Her tone cruelly mimicked mine.

I turned to the full-length mirror on the closet door, tucking in my red blouse. "Anyway, do you remember what she said?"

Linnea sighed and set down her coffee cup with a clunk. "Some damned thing about how Anya's advice would only get her deeper in trouble," she said irritably. "There was something about how she wished she'd never seen the cards. Christ, Sharon, it was just some stupid, superstitious thing. Why am I supposed to remember?"

Because Molly took the trouble to remember your problems, I thought. I slipped on my jacket and arranged the collar of my blouse, gearing up to ask the question I really dreaded.

"Lin, while you were cleaning last night, did you come across that piece of drapery cord I cut off while I was putting up the new curtains?"

"What cord?"

"It was rolled up on the coffee table. A white cord."

"I don't remember it."

"You didn't see it on the coffee table, or any-place else?"

"No. For Christ's sake, Sharon, what's so important about some leftover cord?"

I shrugged. "Maybe I'll turn into one of those old ladies who collects string."

She giggled. "A string-collecting detective who ties up her suspects and makes them confess all."

I smiled, glad her good humor had returned. "It could be a professional asset." I twisted my hair into a loose knot at the nape of my neck and gathered up my bag just as the phone rang.

Linnea answered it. "Hank. He wants you to

come over to All Souls."

"Thanks." As I crossed the room, I said, "Look, Lin, try to take it easy today. Don't think you have to do everything at once."

"Okay." Again, the guilty, little-girl look. It gave me the odd sensation that Linnea had substituted me for the vanished husband as an authority figure, a role I didn't relish at all. The uneasy sensation persisted all through the drive to All Souls and the pretrial conference.

Now I sat at my desk, staring at her message. I knew very little about parenting, and the idea of becoming saddled with a twenty-nine-year-old child was appalling. And what of Linnea's own children, who needed to depend on her? For them, she should become strong and resourceful as she had once been. They couldn't forever be farmed off to Granny.

No, I resolved, Linnea would have to get through the day without me. I would do her more good by putting to rest my suspicions of her involvement in Molly's murder than by coddling her all afternoon. I crumpled her message and tossed it in the basket as I headed for the door.

11

Mr. Moe and Jeffrey Neverman stood on the sidewalk in front of the Albatross Superette, under the sign supplied by our local Seven-Up distributor. A blue van bearing the Sunrise Blind Center's name was parked at the curb. Neverman must be making a delivery too clumsy for Sebastian and Gus.

I pulled the MG into the bus stop across the street and idled there, smiling at the contrast between the two men. Mr. Moe was as dapper as it was possible to be in a long white apron, his hair carefully slicked back, his brown slacks in a knifelike crease. Neverman, on the other hand, wore scruffy faded Levi's and a workshirt whose tattered tails hung out. In daylight, his gray-flecked hair was even shaggier than it had looked last night in the dark of the old church.

A wine distributor's truck pulled up. The driver hopped out and began unloading crates onto the sidewalk. Mr. Moe spoke briefly with him, and then he and Neverman went inside the store.

Early afternoon seemed a bad time to hold a private conversation with my corner grocer. I considered for a moment and, prompted by the horn of a bus that roared up behind me, decided to try to track Sebastian down again. If he wasn't at the Center, I could always take Clemente up on his offer of a tour.

When I got there, though, I realized Clemente might not appreciate my barging in on his residents without permission. It seemed prudent to check with him first. The door of the rectory — a long, low building of the same style as the church — stood open. I went into a lobby that shone with ceramic tiles, chose one of the three dark-wood doors that opened off there, and knocked. Clemente's voice issued an invitation to enter.

The room had gleaming parquet floors, and the bright Mexican rugs Linnea had mentioned hung on the adobe walls. The director sat at a desk in the center, one long leg thrown across its corner. He was eating a cup of yogurt, and he gestured with his spoon when he looked up.

"Sharon! You've come for that tour."

"I had the afternoon off, so I thought I'd let you show me around," I said, assuming Sebastian would show up on the tour.

"Great! Have a seat while I finish my lunch." He motioned at a wicker chair on the other side of the desk.

"You like that stuff?" I asked, pointing at the yogurt.

"It keeps the weight down." He patted the beginnings of a paunch. "Hey, I really like your friend Linnea."

"I'm sure it's mutual. She was telling me what

a fabulous place you have here."

He grinned. "I don't mind it, although it still seems strange, living in a house intended for a priest. I'm sure I have a better time in it than the priests ever did."

"I'll bet," I said, thinking of the waterbed.

Clemente set his spoon in an ashtray and tossed the half-full cup of yogurt in the wastebasket. "God, that makes an awful lunch! I'd have been better off taking Linnea out for Mexican food, which I plan to do as soon as I can get free. She claims the Mexican food in San Diego is unbeatable, but there's this little place I found . . ." His eyes grew serious. "You and she have been friends a long time, haven't you?"

"Since grade school."

"What's her story, anyway? She said something last night about going to the fortune teller because she was willing to try anything. But later she didn't want to talk about it."

"It's nothing so unusual. She was divorced a few months ago and it's a difficult adjustment."

He nodded slowly. "She mentioned her little girls were staying with their grandmother. She came to visit you to get away from it all?"

"And to do some thinking."

"She seems very fond of you."

"Well, we've been friends most of our lives."

"And she seems quite taken with your profession."

"It's natural. She's thought a lot about jobs

100

lately, since she has to decide what she wants to do."

"Would you recommend the life of a private eye?"

"No, not for anyone with a family. The hours are too long and the rewards too uncertain."

"Still, she seems fascinated. You talk to her about your cases?"

Clemente's probing made me uncomfortable. "No. Working for a law firm, most of what I do is confidential. How about that tour now?"

He stood up and, with a deep bow, motioned me toward the door.

"Let me tell you a little about the Center and what we're trying to do here," he said as we walked toward the former convent. "And forgive me if I start to sound like a Gray Line guide. I take friends and relatives of the residents through here several times a week, to say nothing of all sorts of government officials, so my speech can get a little dry and pat." Even as he made his apologies there was a weariness in his tone that told me he'd made this excuse many times before.

"Go ahead. I enjoy a good lecture."

"Great. We've got a philosophy here at the Center that blind people can do almost anything sighted people can, given the proper training. And that's our goal for each resident: to help him become as independent as possible, learn a trade, and eventually move back into the community. All the people here have been blinded recently,

101

so they have a lot of adjustments to make. We attempt to ease them, without coddling or being overprotective."

"How does that approach seem to work?"

"So far, we've had remarkable luck. Of course, we never have more than forty-five residents at a given time, and with a staff of ten counselors, we're able to give each very personalized attention." He stopped at the door of the convent. Bottlebrush bloomed thickly on either side.

"Let me tell you what made me revamp the Center's program in the first place," he went on. "When I first came on board as director, the Center was housed in an old hospital in the Haight-Ashbury. The program was about as innovative as your old-time grammar school. There were rigid rules, limited vocational training, and even a system of bells to tell the residents when to get up, when to eat, when to go to bed."

"And it's not that way now?"

"Damn right it's not."

"When did you change it?"

"Two years ago, after what you might call an electrifying experience." Clemente chuckled, but even that sounded part of a routine. "You see, there was a power failure one night that put the electronically operated bells out. And when the staff came on the next morning, they discovered some of the residents had sat up all night in their chairs because the bells hadn't told them to go to bed."

"Good Lord!"

"You can imagine my shock: We'd squashed all the initiative out of the very people we were supposed to help. I set to redesigning the program immediately. Part of it was to get the hell out of that hospital environment. Fortunately for us, Saint Luke's had caught fire, and given the dwindling number of sisters in the order and the poor shape of the facilities, they decided not to rebuild. So here we are."

It was a fascinating anecdote, but Clemente's flat delivery took the shine from it. I sensed the director was much less than enthusiastic about his work.

"What was your background before you came here?" I asked.

"I worked with ex-cons."

"Doing what?"

"First as director of a halfway house. That closed. Budget cuts. Most of my charges are now back in prison. Next I ran a counseling program for parolees." His lips twisted bitterly. "When they scrapped that, one of my most promising men shot himself, his wife, and two kids."

"I'm sorry." I'd seen social-service personnel like Clemente before — former liberals turned cynics by the system.

"You do what you can." He opened the door of the convent and we went into an entry similar to that of the rectory. Archways led to large rooms on either side, with a wide staircase straight ahead.

Clemente gestured to the left. "This is the

dining hall. It's the focal point of social life at the Center."

The room was filled with square tables covered with white cloths, already laid for dinner with sparkling glass and silverware.

"We've tried to create a homey atmosphere, with small tables and family-style service," Clemente explained. "Our people need to learn to relate to others normally again. The feeling of being an outcast or, in some cases, abhorrence of one's condition, can be diminished by developing friendships with others in the same boat."

He turned to the other archway. "This room will be a lounge when we fix the roof in the church. Right now, it's our workshop, where we make the brushes. We'll move the workshop to the church when it's ready."

The room contained benches — sheets of plywood on sawhorses. On stools around them sat men and women of all ages and races. They cut, twisted, and tied brushes in various stages of completion. Had I not known they were blind, I would have been fooled by the accuracy of their movements.

"Blind people are very well suited to this kind of work," Clemente said. "Their sense of touch is highly developed. We get the materials wholesale, on a procurement contract arranged by the state. Each resident spends three hours a day in the workshop, and the rest of his time is devoted to vocational training."

"What about the other stuff?"

"What stuff?"

"Like the shoelaces and dishwashing gloves Sebastian peddles. Did the state arrange for those too?"

Clemente stared thoughtfully at the worker nearest the door, then stepped forward and peered over his shoulder. "That's good work, Paul." He patted the man's arm and turned back to me. "So Sebastian's been peddling things on the side again, has he?"

"Isn't he supposed to? I'm sorry. I don't want to get him in trouble."

"Oh, it's perfectly okay. He knows his first duty is to keep those racks stocked. And, frankly, I don't care how he sells the stuff as long as it's sold. The revenues help keep this place afloat, since our grants never quite cover expenses." Still, Clemente looked disturbed.

"Will the new merchandise be on the racks soon?" I asked.

"When we get ones that can hold it properly. Sebastian just can't wait — the man's a born entrepreneur."

"I'm interested in Sebastian. What's his background?"

Clemente started toward the staircase. "That's for him to tell you, if he sees fit. I will say that he's been with us since I became director and that he's one of our most able and enthusiastic workers."

"Can you tell me how he was blinded? An explosion, wasn't it?"

"I don't remember every case history," Clemente replied curtly. "We have forty-five people through here every year. I believe it was an explosion at an oil refinery, but I can't be sure."

"Seems I heard something like that too." I followed Clemente upstairs and along the hall, past vocational training and counseling rooms, and then to the third floor where cell-like rooms seemed little changed since the days nuns knelt at their devotions. The convent was stuffy in the afternoon heat, and I was glad when we went back outside after a final tour of the stainless-steel kitchen.

The director accompanied me to the gate on Twenty-fourth Street, chattering about his program's potential and telling me to say hello to Linnea. "I'll call her about that Mexican food. Maybe you and a friend would like to join us?"

"Maybe." I thought briefly about Greg and wondered how he and Clemente would get along. Thanking Herb for the tour, I started off toward my car. When the director had disappeared down the path, however, I slipped back through the gate. He had omitted the former church from his itinerary, and I wanted to look it over in daylight.

He leaned forward. "I believe you *do* know something."

"I said so, didn't I?"

"Where is this unlikely place?"

I shook my head in the negative.

Hood's hand moved toward the phone. "I could call the FBI and let them get it out of you."

"But you won't."

"Why not?"

"Because you have no guarantee I'd cooperate. I could claim I was merely speculating about coming across the gin. And then where would you be?" Inwardly, I willed him to take his hand away from that phone.

"No place." He stood. "Okay, lady, like I said, I like your style. I'll give you a try. Let's play it your way."

"Good. Is there any way to distinguish the shipment?"

"Yes. If the gin had been intended for only one consignee, we'd be out of luck. Fortunately, this was a CFS shipment. That means that cargo for several different consignees was loaded together. To distinguish among them, the cases bear different shipping marks."

I felt a flash of excitement and reached for the notebook where I'd copied the markings from the cases of gin in the Blind Center storeroom. "Shipping marks are pretty distinctive, aren't they?"

"Generally. They can be the entire address of the consignee or abbreviations." Hood hit an intercom and said, "Mary, get me the file on the Tanqueray theft, will you?" He met the secretary at the door and turned, flipping through a manila folder. Standing over me, he read, "Amco, Oakland, PO 1732. Mean anything?"

"No."

"Brothers Wholesale Liquors, San Francisco, PO XX-349-765."

"No."

"Sales Liquor Distributing, Oakland, PO 77886-52-B."

"That's it."

"What?"

"It's your gin, all right."

Hood shut the folder and went back around his desk. He sat, drumming his fingers on the blotter. "Okay, lady, what now?"

"Like I said, I'll tip the FBI."

He motioned at his phone.

"No, I'll call from somewhere else. I need to do some bargaining first."

"You're free to bargain from here."

"No, I do better in private." I stood up, taking out one of my cards. Setting it in front of him, I said, "Remember, that's where to send my check."

21

The phone booth across the street from Circle Wharf and Warehouse was hot and steamy. I propped the door open with my foot while I waited for Greg to come on the line.

"Sharon! It's about time." He sounded like he was gritting his teeth. "You'd better have something good to tell me."

"How about if I were to give you the person who killed Antonio and Neverman — plus made you look good to our local office of the FBI."

"Right. Big talk," he growled. But he sounded hopeful.

"Okay, Gregory." I took a deep breath. "There's an old ironworks at India Basin, near Hunters Point. In the warehouse at the end of the pier, you'll find a lot of gin, close to two containerloads of it. It's stolen, from Circle Wharf and Warehouse in Alameda. If you tip the Feds in a hurry, they might find the thieves there with the stuff."

Greg was silent, but papers shuffled, as if he were making notes.

"Neverman and Antonio were killed because they caught on to the people who plan to fence the gin," I went on. "There's a fencing ring operating right in my neighborhood."

"So who's the killer?"

"I don't know yet."

"You don't . . . all right, Sharon!"

"I said *yet*. I need your help."

"You bet you need help!"

"Greg — give me three hours. It's almost five o'clock now. Call off the cop on my apartment. By eight o'clock you'll have your killer." I hoped my voice sounded more confident than I felt.

He paused. "Goddamn it, Sharon," he said in a low voice. "Do you realize what you're asking of me?"

"I realize. Please, Greg. If you have any respect for me as a professional, please give me the time."

He was silent. Finally he said, "Dammit, Sharon, why I ever wasted all that chocolate on you . . ."

"Does that mean you'll do it?"

"You said three hours?"

"Right."

"Three hours it is. I'll call everyone off. But, Sharon . . ."

"Yes?"

"If you don't deliver, don't expect to work in this state again. Not as a private eye."

His threat, I was certain, was serious, but it did nothing to dampen my spirits. Greg must have faith in my abilities or he wouldn't have given me this chance. "Don't worry. I'll deliver."

I headed for home in the rented Toyota. Bad as our relationship had become in the past two days, there were some questions I had to ask Linnea.

Carrying my mail — a letter from my mother and a request for alumni contributions from the University of California — I banged the apartment door and walked noisily down the hall, trying to act as if nothing had happened the night before. In the archway to the main room, I stopped, surprised.

Linnea stood by the bed, packing her suitcase. It was an orderly suitcase, and Linnea herself looked tidy: She wore a tan pantsuit, and her hair was clean and shining, her makeup carefully applied.

She looked up and said, "I'm going home to San Diego."

I put my mail on the table and sat down. The room was neat, the magazines she'd soaked with liquor the night before laid out to dry. Watney, contented once more, curled in the center of the bed.

"When did you decide this?" I asked.

"This morning. The kids have been with Mama long enough. I miss them, and it's time we had a home of our own again."

I couldn't keep the incredulous look off my face.

"I know it's a shock." Linnea laughed nervously and shut the suitcase. "The last time you see me, I'm sloppy drunk, blubbering about how the world's treated me, and now . . ." She sat in the chair across from me, looking uncertain.

189

"Listen, Sharon," she went on, "I'm sorry for all the trouble I've caused you, and I hope it hasn't damaged our friendship, not permanently."

"I . . ." I shook my head in confusion. "I . . . no, of course it hasn't. But you must admit this is a startling transformation. What happened?"

She laughed nervously again. "Oh, you know how people have moments of truth. I guess you could say I had mine last night."

"Will you tell me about it?"

"Sure. Why not?" She sat back, smoothing her carefully pressed trousers. "You see, I was awfully upset when you walked out of here. Nobody had ever spoken to me like that. Not Mama, not Jim, or anybody. Why, when Jim left me, he barely said a thing — his lawyer did all the talking. You really pulled the rug out from under me."

"And that shaped you up?"

"No. In fact, it made things worse. I . . . I decided to kill myself."

"God, no!"

"Oh, yes." She nodded solemnly. "It was the whole big horror show: razor blade, bathtub full of warm water, and me, clutching the last bottle of booze in the house. And I couldn't do it. I was scared you wouldn't come back and find me in time. Can you imagine: me, who always despised fakers, doing the fakiest thing of all?"

I glanced at her wrists. No bandages. None of the little hesitation marks suicide attempts left.

"Anyway," Linnea went on, "I realized what

190

a total fraud I was when that cop came to the door. I lay there in the bathtub, thinking it was you and that maybe you'd forgotten your key. I pictured you getting Tim to open the door, and how shocked and sorry you'd be. But the cop kept on pounding, and finally I had to get out of the tub and answer. Then when he said Madame Anya had been murdered . . . oh, wow!"

"So what did you do?"

"Got angry at myself. I kept thinking about what you'd said — that at least I had life, even if I didn't have much else. That life hasn't been worth much to me for a long time now, and I hated myself so much for being such a cowardly fake that I said, 'Okay, take your lousy life and gamble with it.' "

"What?"

"That's right. Do you remember how we used to ask the cards a question?"

I nodded. The solitaire game we'd played back in San Diego.

"I decided I would play one game," Linnea said. "And the question would be: 'Do I live and work things out?' If the game came out, I'd try. If not . . ." She slashed a finger across one wrist.

I pressed my hands to my face, shivering. The odds against the game coming out in one try were incredibly high.

Linnea went on, "Anyway, to cut the melodrama short, I played the game, and it came out. And when it did, I realized I had to face up to things and take my life in hand whether I liked it or not. Because I'd been so lucky, so blessed . . . Sharon!"

I was crying, tears leaking through my fingers and trickling down the backs of my hands. My entire body shook.

"Shar, don't! It's okay. The game came out. And I honestly don't think I would have shaped up without the shock of . . . oh, hey, come on!"

Linnea moved to the arm of my chair, her hands on my heaving shoulders. "Hey, don't! Everything's all right."

I wished I could believe her. Giving in to this sudden reversal of roles, I buried my wet face against my friend.

When I had calmed down, Linnea went back to her chair and lit a cigarette. Her motions were measured. I could scarcely fathom such a change in less than twenty-four hours.

With my fit of tears behind me, I felt better, though. Too much tension held in check for too long had worn me down.

Linnea said, "Wow, you really came apart for a few minutes there. It can't all be because of me. What else is bothering you?"

"The image of you floating in a bathtub of bloody water is enough to unhinge anybody."

"Maybe, but there's something besides that."

She was too calm, too dispassionate, for Linnea. I knew this wouldn't last, but it was a step forward. If I could get her back to San Diego and her kids while she was still in this frame of mind, she might work things out after all.

She asked, "It's the murders, isn't it? Molly and Madame Anya?"

"Yes," I admitted. "You think you're hardened, you think you've seen a lot, and then . . ." I shook my head.

"I'm sorry," Linnea said quietly. "Did they find any clues yet?"

"No. I've got three hours — less now — to come up with something, or I'm likely to end up in jail for obstructing a police investigation."

Linnea's eyes widened. "You're kidding!"

"I don't think Greg would go so far as to arrest me, but . . ."

"What're you going to do?"

"Right now, wash my face and change my clothes and go talk to some people."

"You ought to eat something."

I motioned wearily. "I couldn't."

"Sharon, you've got to start eating better."

Who else had told me that? Stanley, the bartender. It reminded me of the questions I had to ask Linnea. "Hey," I said, "have you heard from Herb Clemente?"

She smiled. "Yes, I called him this morning to apologize for freaking out on the phone. He had to go to LA today, but he said he'd be back sometime this evening. If he's here early enough, he's going to drive me to the airport."

"Why'd he go to LA, do you know?"

"No. He just said on business."

Blind Center business? Or something to do with

193

fencing a load of Tanqueray gin?

"When's your flight?" I asked.

"Eleven was the earliest I could get. If Herb doesn't call, I'll take a cab."

"No, I'll try to be here to drive you."

"If you don't show, it'll mean you're in trouble. I'll stay and try to help."

I smiled weakly. "Thanks. Another question: the other day when Molly was in here, around five o'clock the day she died . . ."

Linnea flushed. "What about it?"

"I'm not interested in your conversation. Anyway, I think I know what it was about."

"I'm sure you do. She was yelling at me for drinking so much. What about that day?"

"When Gus and Sebastian came over here from Mr. Moe's, did Gus come inside the apartment?"

Linnea frowned. "I think . . . yeah, I'm sure he did."

"All the way inside?"

"As a matter of fact, yes. He sat right where you are now and looked through some magazines on the table. Why?"

I ignored her question. Gus had had the opportunity to take the cord. He also had had the opportunity to strangle Molly — none of the domino players had given him an airtight alibi. All along I'd discounted Gus because I'd thought him too stupid. But what if it was an act? Gus worked for the Blind Center; he had told Tim this morning that he had plenty of money to pay the rent. Gus could be part of the fencing scheme.

194

"Why?" Linnea insisted.

"What?"

"Why do you ask about Gus?"

"It has something to do with my missing drapery cord."

"Are you still on the string-collecting jag?"

"Why not? It's a hobby I could keep up in jail."

"You know, that's not really funny."

"I know." I grabbed my bag and, since I'd left my .38 locked in the glovebox of my car at the airport, went to the strongbox and took out the other one I kept there.

Linnea stared at the gun. "Hey, I thought you wanted to change your clothes."

"Nope. I've lost too much time as is. I'm going over to Mr. Moe's."

"I'll come along with you and pick up some wine. I drank everything."

"No."

Linnea looked reproachfully at me. "Sharon, all I want is a glass of wine. I'm over swilling it down, believe me."

"What I meant was, it could get unpleasant at the Superette." I paused, remembering the wine I'd left with Stanley the other night. "I know where there's a bottle of Grey Riesling, though. Go over to Ellen T's and ask Stanley for it. It belongs to me."

"You do leave things in the most peculiar places. Let's go."

Halfway down the front steps, I said, "Oh, by

the way, I thought of filing a complaint about the way Greg Marcus hassled you yesterday, but first I want to take it up with him personally. Do you have any choice words to pass along?"

Linnea stopped at the foot of the stairs. "Greg Marcus? The guy who sends you all the chocolate? The cop who was here last night?"

"Yes."

"What about him?"

"He came over and upset you. Remember how he kept asking you what Molly gave you for safe-keeping? When you threw the chocolates he brought at him?"

She shook her head. "Sharon, that wasn't Greg Marcus. I mean, all he did was leave the box of candy outside the door. I never even laid eyes on him until last night."

"Who was it, then? Who upset you?"

"Sebastian, the guy who peddles the brushes. He got me to let him in on the excuse that you'd ordered a toilet brush."

I remembered it, lying on the floor among the candies.

"*Sebastian* wanted to know what Molly had left with you?"

Bewildered, she nodded. "But it's okay, really. He came by today and apologized. He said he was worried about Gus's inheritance, or he wouldn't have been so rude."

"Gus's inheritance? Linnea, are you sure Gus was in here, by the coffee table the other afternoon?"

"Yes. Sharon, what . . ."

"Listen, go back inside and lock the door and stay there."

"What? Can't I even get the wine?"

I hesitated. "Oh, all right, get it. But then come back and don't let anybody in."

"What about Herb?"

"Definitely *not*. Tell him you'll meet him at the Blind Center later. Stall him a while. But I don't want anybody coming in that apartment until I get back from Mr. Moe's. Do you understand?"

"Okay. Don't get all excited. I'll hold the fort."

"Good." I hurried toward the corner. As I waited for the light, I watched Linnea cross in mid-block to Ellen T's. Her hands were thrust deep in the pockets of her jacket, and her head was bowed dejectedly. In the fog that had followed the day's rain, she looked lost and alone.

I glanced up and down the street, patting the reassuring bulk of the .38 in my bag. With its help, I'd get the answers I needed out of Mr. Moe.

22

Mr. Moe was stacking oranges in the produce case when I entered. His eyes jerked to me in the slanting mirror above the display. Under his trembling hand, the top orange teetered and bounced to the floor, bringing the rest of the pyramid down after it.

The grocer gave a dismayed cry and dropped to his knees. He scrambled around, filling his arms with fruit. I made no move to help him.

"Jumpy lately, aren't you, Mr. Moe?"

He rocked back on his heels and looked up, hugging the oranges. "What do you want of me now?"

"I'm a customer, Mr. Moe. You don't want to send me off to Safeway to spend my money."

He sighed and let his arms drop, releasing the oranges. Indifferent to them, he got to his feet, brushing dust from his trousers. "What is it you need?"

"Some gin. Tanqueray gin, to be exact."

A muscle twitched in his cheek. "I am sorry. I do not have a license to sell hard liquor. I have only beer and wine."

"What happened to that case of gin you had in your stockroom last night — the one that the

198

bottle you broke came from?"

"I am sorry. . . ."

I made a big show of examining the wines on the shelf behind the counter. "Come now, Mr. Moe, you couldn't have broken all those bottles. Although you really should be more careful about dropping things." I motioned at the oranges on the floor.

"Miss McCone, I stock no such thing."

"Of course you don't!" I whirled on him. "You have no such item because it's already in the storeroom at the Blind Center. But when are the thieves making their next drop — the thieves you met at India Basin last night?"

His body sagged. "That was you?"

"At India Basin? Yes."

"And you know everything?"

"I know about the fencing operation. And the big gin heist. And that this store is a drop for goods on their way to the Blind Center. By the way, do you know Clemente has skipped town?"

"A business trip to Los Angeles is not what you call 'skipping town.' "

"A hastily manufactured trip, wasn't it? What's he doing there? Waiting to see if the whole operation falls apart? If it doesn't, he returns quietly. If it does, he runs. The Mexican border is an easy two hours drive."

The grocer shook his head stubbornly. "You do not understand."

"I understand more than you think. For example, I understand there are other drops, at other grocery stores in the neighborhood."

He began to pace up and down the aisle. "What is it you want from me? What is it?"

"Just some straight answers, for a change. How do you coordinate all those drops so Neverman knows when to pick up the merchandise?"

"I can see you will not give up." He plucked a loaf of soft white bread from a shelf, and his slender fingers squeezed it rhythmically.

"No, I won't give up. The fencing operation has fallen apart. The FBI is probably at India Basin now. You may as well tell me about it." As I spoke, I stared in fascination at Mr. Moe's hands. They squeezed the bread until it hung limp, doubled over.

The grocer's eyes followed mine to the strangled loaf. "What am I doing?" he exclaimed. He hurled the bread back on the shelf and flung his arms wide above his head. "What *am* I doing?" He tried to push past me, but I blocked him.

"No, Mr. Moe," I said. "You're not going near the cash register."

"What is wrong? Why not?"

"Because you have a gun stashed behind that counter. All the local grocers do." I brought out my own, holding it at waist level, where it couldn't be seen from outside the store.

Mr. Moe stared at the weapon. His tongue darted over his dry lips.

I said, "Lock the door, pull the shades, and we'll talk."

He did as I told him. I motioned him over

against the freezers. "Now tell me how you co-ordinated the pickups from the drops."

The grocer folded his arms over his chest. "The gun is not necessary. I will tell you. It does not matter now."

"I feel better with the gun between us. Talk."

"Sebastian coordinated the pickups."

"Oh, come on!"

"No, that was his real job for the Center. When he came in to restock the racks, the grocers would tell him if there was merchandise to be picked up. When he returned to the Center, he would relay this information to Neverman. Sebastian has an excellent memory — I believe he perfected it by memorizing racing forms before he went blind."

"And Gus — what was his part?"

The grocer shrugged. "He led Sebastian."

It was probably a larger role than that. "All right. And for acting as your courier, Clemente allowed Sebastian to stay on at the Blind Center. And gave him so little money he was forced to steal already stolen goods and peddle them on the side."

Mr. Moe's eyes widened indignantly. "That is not so! Sebastian had fifty thousand dollars invested in the operation. We all had some money tied up in it."

"But not as much as Sebastian."

He was silent.

I thought of Sebastian's settlement from Standard Oil. He'd said he lost it in a bad investment.

The fencing operation was the worst he could have chosen. "Tell me how this all came about."

Mr. Moe hesitated, staring at my gun. "When Sebastian was first referred to the Center, Clemente took a liking to him. They held long conversations while Clemente taught him to play chess by touch. Finally, Clemente announced he wanted to take Sebastian into our scheme. He felt it wise to have a patient involved, who could report if any of the other patients became suspicious. And, of course, Sebastian had fifty thousand dollars that we could use to finance our purchases."

"So Sebastian gave Clemente his money."

"Yes."

"And, in turn, received a share of the profits."

Mr. Moe was silent again.

"Oh, so he *didn't* receive any money. That was why he stole. He'd invested all he had, and you people used it as capital and didn't return a cent."

"I admit it was not fair. But he did receive food and shelter. And we paid him back."

"When?"

"Today."

I recalled Clemente and Neverman discussing paying back a loan. "Why did you people suddenly decide to return his investment?"

"Sebastian demanded it, as soon as he heard of the gin purchase. He said he would leave us alone if he got it, but otherwise he would go to the police. We wanted him to leave — his actions lately had been strange. He took things, as you said. He was a risk we could not afford."

A lot of people had threatened to go to the police in the last few days. Sebastian was lucky he hadn't ended up dead. I said, "So Clemente paid Sebastian off."

"This morning he gave him a cashier's check for the full amount. That is why Clemente had to fly to Los Angeles: to make arrangements for the disposal of the gin. You see, to pay Sebastian, he had to borrow from the Blind Center funds."

Tampering with federal funds was no laughing matter. Clemente would want to replace the fifty thousand quickly.

"All right," I said, "now I want to know how this whole thing got started. It can't have been going on any longer than the Blind Center's been here. How'd you get connected with these folks, Mr. Moe?"

His hooded eyes shifted away from me. "How?"

"Before he went to prison Neverman used to sell his overloads to me. Not very often, though. I was never a big dealer, and after he was arrested I became frightened and stopped altogether. Naturally we did no business when he returned. He could not find a job. No trucking firm would hire him."

"But then the Blind Center relocated here, and Neverman renewed his acquaintance with his old counselor, Clemente. With your help, they developed their fencing scheme."

"No, they came to me with the complete plan.

I blame it all on Neverman. Herb Clemente is not a bad man. I do not think he intended to become so deeply involved. But after years in social service, a man becomes cynical and desperate. He does things he never dreamed he would and thinks nothing of it because he has seen much greater evil."

It was probably true, but I ignored his amateur psychoanalysis. "Neverman put you in touch with Clemente, then. You and your grocer friends were to be a buffer between thieves and the Blind Center, so it wouldn't get around that the Center was receiving."

"It was best it not become commonly known."

"That's why you left Neverman outside when you contacted the people at India Basin last night."

"Yes, but Neverman ruined that when he shouted and ran after you. They saw the truck and realized who they were dealing with."

I nodded. "And the thieves will spill that to the Feds. It's all over for you people. Now let's get to those killings."

Mr. Moe's head jerked. Fear shone in his eyes. "I know nothing of those."

"Don't you? Didn't Molly Antonio tell Clemente she knew he was fencing because she found evidence in an item Sebastian sold her? Didn't Clemente tell you to kill her, that night when you supposedly went to deliver groceries?"

"No! He never said anything to me. I did not know she had accused him." Mr. Moe's eyes darted wildly to the gun and back to my face. "You must believe me! I went merely to deliver her food. Would I be so stupid as to leave the groceries there if I had killed her?"

Maybe, but I doubted it. "What about Neverman, then? I imagine Clemente can make him do anything he cares to."

Mr. Moe gestured weakly. "I . . . I do not know."

"His wife, whom he hated, was the next one killed."

"She was forcing him to go back to her. Clemente said he must. Neverman was furious, but I do not think he would have killed her. In time, he would have been able to deal with her, to work something out."

"He certainly did."

Mr. Moe shuddered. "I know nothing of it."

"You can't get off that easily, Mr. Moe," I said with a flash of anger. "You're in this thing all the way. You can be charged as an accessory. . . ."

The outside door of the stockroom slammed.

I motioned for Mr. Moe to remain quiet.

Footsteps came across the room.

Gesturing with my gun, I marched Mr. Moe toward the swinging door. He walked stiffly, like a robot.

The swinging door opened, and Neverman looked in. His eyes widened, and he bolted.

I shoved the grocer out of my way and went after Neverman. He dodged through the stacked-up crates and disappeared. An engine roared. As I burst through the outer door, the blue van pulled away.

I went back inside. Mr. Moe leaned against the counter, nursing a bumped knee. His body dropped, totally defeated.

I put my gun away.

"What will you do with me now?" the grocer asked.

"Nothing. You're not going anywhere."

He acknowledged it with a bow of his head. "I have nowhere to go."

"Neverman won't get far, either. He was helping the thieves deliver the rest of the gin, wasn't he?"

"Yes. Speed was of the essence, and they knew who they were dealing with, so we had nothing to lose."

"He'll probably go back to India Basin, straight into an FBI trap."

Mr. Moe remained silent, rubbing his knee.

I moved toward the door.

"You are leaving me?"

"You won't be alone for long." I turned the lock and went out.

By the time I reached the curb, the double lock on the door clicked into place behind me. When I got to Ellen T's, I looked back. The light that had streamed around the drawn shades of the Superette went out.

23

Ellen T's was packed with drinkers getting started on the weekend a day early. I waved to Stanley and called, "Is Gus around?"

"In the back room." He motioned toward the rear, where the pool and the domino players congregated.

The two halves of the room back there were divided by an invisible gulf of time. To the left, the young pool players strutted about, guzzling beer from the bottle and eyeing one another's shots. They wore tight jeans and T-shirts, with the inevitable bunch of keys hooked to the belt loops. The keys, a young Latino had once told me, showed a man's standing in the community; a large number on the ring indicated he had access to and responsibility for a great many worldly places.

To my right sat the domino players: old men in khaki pants and plaid shirts, who sipped slowly at their frosty mugs and contemplated their moves in silence. Their monosyllabic conversation was drowned out from time to time by shouts from the pool players, but if they resented them, they didn't betray it by so much as a glance.

Gus slouched over a table with three other men,

his jowls resting on his balled fists as he studied the white-dotted rectangles in front of him. It might be the night before his wife's funeral, but he had not deviated from his routine.

I went up and put a hand on his arm.

"Miss McCone!" he exclaimed. "What . . ."

"I need to talk to you, Gus."

"I'm right in the middle of a game."

"Please — it's important."

He shot a long-suffering glance around the table. "What say we take a break, boys?"

They grumbled, but nodded assent. Gus followed me to the front room, clutching his beer. We sat at a table near the door.

"What's wrong?" Gus asked. "Nobody else died, did they?"

"No, thank God. I have a couple of questions for you."

"Will it take long? I'm ahead in that game, and I don't want any of those guys messing with my dominoes while my back's turned."

"It won't take long at all. The other day you came into my apartment to wait for Molly and took some cord off the table."

"I what?"

"You know you did, Gus. You take a lot of things, like the ashtray from Tim's bookcase this morning."

He colored. "How did you know?"

"Never mind. I know why Molly threw you out, though. And I know you steal brushes off Sebastian's parka."

Shamed, he stared down into his beer mug. Finally he said, "I try. I try all the time, but I can't help it." Suddenly, he glanced at the back room. "You won't tell them, will you? They don't know. They think I'm just a regular guy."

"All I'm interested in is that cord. What did you do with it?"

"Didn't do nothing with it."

"Do you have it now?"

"Uh, no."

"Where is it?"

"Well, I . . ."

"Gus, where?"

"Well, I had it in my jacket pocket. And I took it out and sort of fiddled with it while I was walking Sebastian back to the Blind Center for dinner."

"And?"

"Sebastian, he's sharp. He felt me fiddling with it, and he asked me what it was. He claims something comes over my voice when I've stolen stuff. He can always tell. Anyway, he made me admit what I'd done, and then he took the cord away from me. Said he'd take it back to your place, and you'd never have to know it'd been gone."

But he hadn't returned it. He had taken it to the Center.

"Okay. Another question. How well did you know Anya Neverman?"

He frowned. "Pretty well. She was Molly's best friend. And Sebastian and me used to stop up there and sell her stuff. He was trying to make a deal to sell her all her candles and lucky charms if he could get them."

"When you went to see her, did she always answer the door with her gun in her hand?"

"Of course. Anya was a little cracked. Always thought somebody was gonna rape her. Even her own husband didn't want to do that." He snickered.

Annoyed, I said, "Well, her fears weren't so silly after all. Someone *did* kill her."

He sobered instantly. "You're right. Somebody did. I guess that's worse than rape, isn't it?"

"I would say so. What did you think of Anya's having a gun?"

"Oh, I used to joke with her about it. Called her Anya Oakley. She didn't like that none."

I stared at him. He'd had the motive, the opportunity. But did he have the brains — especially to lie about that cord? "Wait here, Gus." I hurried up to the bar and caught Stanley's eye. "Can you tell me if my friend Linnea picked up the wine?"

Stanley filled a beer mug. "Yeah, she did. A long time ago. Wasn't she out back?"

"Out back where?"

"Watching the domino players. She came in right behind Sebastian and Gus. Gus invited her to watch the game."

"She wasn't there when I arrived."

Gus came up and tugged at my sleeve. "She only stayed for a little while," he said. "Then she decided to walk Sebastian back to the Center.

I thought he might like coming here, but it wasn't much fun for him."

"I thought Sebastian lived with you now."

"He's moving tomorrow if we can get Neverman and the truck."

"Did my friend say why she was going to the Center?"

"She asked if Mr. Clemente was back from LA, and Sebastian said yes. So she decided she'd take Sebastian there and have Mr. Clemente bring her back to pick up her bags on the way to the airport. She going someplace?"

His words were lost to me as I rushed from the bar.

Damn Linnea! Just when I thought she was reliable . . .

I ran across two lanes of traffic to the island in the middle of Guerrero and waited for more cars to clear. As I tore across the other two lanes and down the sidewalk, my feet beat out a refrain:

Not my friend. He can't kill my friend.

The sidewalks of Twenty-fourth Street were empty; the fog and dampness following the rain had driven people inside. I saw them, in the windows of the bars and cafes, warm and safe and unafraid.

As I ran, fragments of long-forgotten prayers echoed in my mind: Let her be all right. Please let her be all right. If she is, I'll be so good.

The iron gate to the church grounds stood open. I stopped.

Quietly, Sharon. As quietly as you can.

I went up the walk. All I heard were traffic sounds from the street. Hopefully, they would cover my approach. I moved to the side door of the church.

At the bottom of the basement stairs, broken glass crunched under my feet. The sweet odor of Riesling drifted up.

I'd come to the right place.

Taking out my gun, I slipped down the hall. An eerie light burned in Neverman's room, a sheet of white that spread across the ceiling. It came from his torch, which, along with the books and ashtray, had been knocked from the crate.

Had Linnea turned on the torch, struggled with him, and escaped? I crept down the hall toward the steps to the vestibule, where another light shone, and listened. Silence hung heavy upstairs.

They might be up there, each hiding from the other in the dark. Or Linnea could have fled. . . .

A thump. Another thump. A dragging sound. More silence.

Any sound from me would tip him off to my presence. I slipped down the hall and back outside. The situation called for reinforcements.

Stuffing my gun in my bag, I hurried down the walk to the street and ran across to one of the cafes where all the safe, happy people were. I forced my way through the crowd to the bar and demanded to use the phone.

"There's a pay phone by the johns, lady."

"I don't have change. I don't have time."

"Look, lady . . ."

"The phone!" I flashed the photostat of my license at the bartender. It wasn't a police shield, but it was damned official looking. His eyes widened, and he handed the phone across the bar.

I dialed the main police number, asked for Communications, listened to a lot of clicks and static on the line. The bartender leaned across at me, his eyes greedy with curiosity. I motioned him away, but he stayed.

The last thing I wanted was a whole bar full of people surging across the street to watch the fun. I searched my memory for the police code numbers Greg had taught me one idle Sunday when we'd had nothing better to do.

"Communications, Lucke."

I identified myself and gave the location of the Blind Center, turning my back on the inquisitive bartender.

"I've got a ten-thirty-one and need assistance. *Quiet* assistance. If the guy hears, it will set him off."

"I'll get it on the air."

Code 10-31 was Homicide in Progress.

I hadn't been sure the cop would cooperate with a civilian, but he must have figured I knew what I was talking about.

I slammed the receiver down and pushed back outside. Depending on its location, a radio car could be here in three or four minutes. Meanwhile, I'd do what I could do to impede the progress of the homicide.

24

I entered the church the way I had before and crept down the hall toward the vestibule. Silence pounded down on me as I mounted the steps. Then I heard scuffling in the main part of the church.

"Please turn on the lights!" Linnea's voice was raw with terror. "Please! I can't see!"

At least she was still alive!

The killer chuckled roughly.

The church was dark except for a bulb in the vestibule. Without light my gun was useless. I crossed to the archway and looked down the aisle, but all I saw was the faint glow of the stained-glass window. Linnea sobbed brokenly.

I slid my hand along the wall to the dimmer switch Neverman had played with two nights ago. It was a risk, but one I'd have to take. Rotating it a fraction of an inch, I watched the lights come up, bathing the altar with their pale-yellow glow.

Linnea cried out.

She and Sebastian were on their knees on the raised platform. He crouched behind her, his left arm hooked around her neck. His right clutched the gun he'd taken from Anya's apartment.

Sebastian's loss of sight was total, as the personnel man at Standard Oil had told me. He couldn't even distinguish between light and shadow. I rotated the switch some more.

Linnea gasped and struggled.

"Don't be afraid," Sebastian said, still oblivious to the change.

I would have shot him then, but I was out of range. Slowly, I started down the aisle.

Linnea saw me. She jerked violently.

"No, no," crooned Sebastian.

I made a levelling motion with my hands, to signal that Linnea should keep calm.

She stared at me with fear-blanked eyes. Given her instability, could I count on her to help?

After about fifteen seconds, she dipped her chin slightly.

Yes, I understand.

I went down the aisle.

"You killed them both, didn't you?" Linnea's voice was less hysterical and very loud.

Good girl. If she kept talking, it would cover my approach.

"I had to."

"Why? Why did you have to?"

"I had to keep them from going to the police. All I wanted was my money back. But Molly, she sent Gus to the Laundromat and told me she had found out we were selling stolen goods. She said she wanted to get my side of the story before she told the cops."

"So you *killed* her?"

"They'd promised to give me my money back

215

after they moved the gin. If she told the cops, it would have blown the whole deal. That money was my only way out of here. I snuck back there that night to try to reason with her. She wouldn't listen. I had a cord in my pocket." As he spoke, his voice picked up speed and the words began to slur together.

"And next you killed Madame Anya." Linnea's eyes were intent on mine as I slipped into the second row of pews. This story could make little sense to her, but she kept him talking anyway.

"Neverman wouldn't go back to her. I knew she'd turn us in, just for spite. I sat downstairs in Gus's apartment thinking how mad she'd be when she figured out he wasn't coming. I went up there, and she answered the door. She sounded crazy. I couldn't handle her."

"You certainly did handle her, you monster! You *strangled* her!"

It was the wrong thing to say. Sebastian jerked Linnea around, pressing her body close to his. I couldn't see the gun.

"I'm no monster! All I wanted was my money!"

Linnea spoke, but her voice was muffled against Sebastian's chest.

"Don't you see?" he asked. "It's nothing against you. But if they find you in Neverman's room shot with his own wife's gun, they'll be sure he did all three murders. You shouldn't have grabbed that flashlight and fought with me down there and run away. It'd be all over by now if you hadn't."

216

Linnea's petite body shuddered. I could see the tremors from where I knelt behind the pews.

"You'll never get away with this!" Hysteria broke through into Linnea's voice. "Someone'll hear the shot!"

"Noise doesn't carry from here to the dormitory."

"Herb . . ."

"Clemente's still in Los Angeles."

"You lied to me!" Linnea struggled against him. "You planned this all along!"

I braced my arms on the back of the pew, aiming my gun and waiting for a chance.

"It's nothing against you," Sebastian repeated. "I'd rather it was your detective friend. She knows too much."

Linnea struggled more wildly. She seemed to have forgotten help was there. "You're crazy! You're a crazy old bastard!"

I heard a sound in the vestibule. The police. Sebastian heard it too.

His head cocked, and he hooked his left arm around Linnea. He jammed the gun to her temple and stood, dragging her up with him.

If I shot now, his reflex would put the bullet through her head.

"Who's there?" Sebastian shouted. "Who's out there?"

All was still.

Linnea's frantic eyes pleaded with mine.

I got up and stood in the aisle, feeling absurdly like the little girl who had played pantomime

217

games with her at long ago birthday parties.

Not yet.

I held up my hands.

When I nod . . .

I mouthed the words. Nodded emphatically.

You . . .

Pointed to her.

Go limp.

Mimicked a faint.

Went through the whole charade once more.

Comprehension in Linnea's eyes.

Sebastian standing, head up like an animal in the forest.

"I know someone's here. Who are you?"

I knelt, once more clasping my gun in both hands, arms braced on the back of the pew. The police presence in the vestibule felt heavy behind me, but no one came to my aid.

Steadying the gun, I took a last look at Linnea.

She nodded, ever so slightly.

Ready.

I took a breath. Waited a few seconds. Nodded.

Linnea went limp.

Sebastian's gun was deflected upward.

I fired.

The shot split the silence, and Sebastian fell, taking Linnea with him.

I stood, jamming the gun in my bag, and ran to help my friend. She rolled off the altar and burrowed into my arms. The church was suddenly filled with uniformed officers.

I couldn't look at Sebastian, but I sensed he

was dead. Taking no chances, I'd aimed to kill.

Keeping my arms around Linnea, I led her up the aisle. At the top, Greg waited, an odd mixture of pride and anxiety on his face. Linnea stumbled and sobbed, but I held on tight. When we met Greg, he opened his arms and encircled us both. I clung to him and Linnea, safe in the knowledge that I'd won my battle against the death of friendship — twice.

25

I glanced at my watch and then at the door of the airport bar.

Greg said, "Jesus Christ, Sharon. Linnea's only been gone four minutes. It probably takes that long even to *find* the ladies' room."

I frowned. "If you're that unconcerned about her, how come you know it's been exactly four minutes?"

He smiled and covered my hand with his. "Take it easy."

"I just want to get her on that plane."

His fingers tightened on mine.

I sipped my wine and stared out the window at a 747 lumbering by. It had been a rough two days, what with the publicity and untangling of red tape. Even though half a dozen cops had witnessed my justifiable homicide, there still had been plenty of red tape.

"Greg," I said after a moment, "I think it's time I moved."

"Maybe."

"The building absolutely drips gloom. The neighborhood too. Sebastian's dead. Mr. Moe hung himself." I shuddered, remembering the newspaper descriptions of the grocer's body hanging in his stockroom. "Clemente got shot resisting arrest here at the airport, and they don't know whether he'll be paralyzed or not."

"And Neverman's a two-time loser," Greg added, "which means he'll get out on parole, screw up again, and be in a third time for good."

"All in a few days' work," I said bitterly.

Greg squeezed my hand. "Goes with the territory."

"That doesn't mean I have to like it."

"Nor I." He paused. "At least you can afford to move if you want. The check from Circle Wharf and Warehouse was very generous."

John Hood had delivered it in person yesterday. "Yes, but I hate to spend it on movers."

"Well, think about it."

"What I'd rather spend it on is a vacation . . ."

Linnea reentered the bar, her hair smoothed and lipstick freshened. She sat down at the table and sipped at her Perrier with lime.

Apparently she noted my approving glance at her drink, because she said, "Yeah. I want to be sober when I see my kids."

"I'll bet they'll be glad you're back."

"They sure will. They need a mother and a home of their own. The latter may take some time."

Greg asked, "What do you plan to do?"

"I've been thinking about that. Once upon a time I was a damned good newswoman. I might approach the TV station I used to work for about a job."

"What do you think your chances are?"

She shrugged. "I don't know, given the job market."

I said, "You know, San Francisco's a good town for women in broadcasting. If it doesn't work out in San Diego, you could always come up and stay with me while you interview the local stations."

Linnea grinned. "It takes a certain amount of courage to extend that invitation, given what I did to your life these past few weeks. I appreciate it."

"Well," Greg said, "no one ever accused Sharon of being without courage. Common sense, maybe."

I glared. "I caught your killer, didn't I?"

"And almost got Linnea killed."

"But she wasn't, was she?"

"You're lucky you still have a license."

"You're lucky you still have a badge!"

"The only reason that was ever in jeopardy is because I listened to you."

"Stop fighting!" Linnea ordered.

The corner of Greg's mouth twitched. "Sharon, will we ever exist in harmony?"

"I'm not sure I want to. Arguing with you is a challenge."

"Speaking of challenges," Linnea said, "I want to know how you figured out Sebastian was the killer. You said you knew it was him when you called the cops and asked for quiet assistance, but how?"

"It wasn't easy, but I had some clues. Clemente had told me that blind people can do almost anything sighted people can, given the proper training. Sebastian had received plenty of that. The killer had to know Anya had a gun in her table in order to take it. Sebastian had heard Gus joke with Anya about it. And Sebastian himself tipped me to an important fact."

"Which was?"

"He said he could get around places he knew perfectly well with the aid of his cane. The places he knew included the Blind Center, the streets and alleys of the neighborhood, and my apartment building."

"Ah hah." Linnea nodded.

"I only wish I'd listened more carefully — and sooner," I added.

"You put it together in enough time." Greg looked at his watch. "Your flight's about to leave, Linnea."

We passed through the security check and walked down the concourse in silence. At the gate, Linnea hugged us and then hurried toward the plane, as if afraid she'd change her mind. Greg and I leaned on the railing watching the other passengers board.

"Well, papoose," he said, "what now?"

"Now?"

"With us."

I glanced at him. His face was serious, without any trace of his characteristic mockery.

"I don't know. We'll see."

"It takes time for two people like us to build a relationship."

"That it does."

"I'm willing to wait, but in the meantime . . ." He fished in his trenchcoat pocket and tossed an object at me.

I caught it. What else? Nestle's Crunch chocolate bar.

12

The church was locked. I started down the path to the side door. Suddenly it opened. I ducked behind a bottlebrush bush.

Neverman came out, in a rush. He crossed the lawn to the rectory and disappeared inside. I waited a minute before I came out of hiding.

The basement was cold, with a dank smell of dry rot that I hadn't noticed the night before. I went along, glancing into the storerooms that opened off the hallway. They were stacked with raw materials for the brushes: plastic and wooden handles, rolls of wire, straw and nylon bristles. The last room, closest to the stairway to the vestibule, was crammed with cardboard cartons. I checked an open box near the door. Shoelaces, like the ones Sebastian had shown me yesterday.

I thought back to Clemente's agitation when I had told him Sebastian was peddling these. Was it possible Sebastian had taken the items without Clemente's permission and pocketed the money? It didn't strike me as likely, but then, I didn't know the brush man very well.

I went on upstairs. The walls of the vestibule were water-stained and flaking away in big chunks. Inside the church, the elements had taken a similar toll: The pews closest to the gaping hole in the roof were in bad condition, and the parquet floor buckled. I stood, caught by the kaleidoscopic pattern of the round stained-glass window above the altar.

Why had Clemente let the church deteriorate so? It would take more talent than Neverman possessed to make it habitable now. I took a last look around and started back to the basement. A sound arrested me on the landing, and I froze.

Sebastian came out of the first storeroom, a shopping bag in his hand. It was heaped with shoelaces, dishwashing gloves, sponges, and wooden spoons. The brush man had expanded his line in a big way. I wondered how he'd explain it when Clemente confronted him.

With his white cane, Sebastian expertly tapped away toward the side door. I remained still until I heard it shut. By the time I got there and peeked out, Sebastian had crossed the lawn toward the rectory. Instead of going in, however, he skirted it, keeping close to the bottlebrush bushes. Suddenly he paused and cocked his head. I watched, safe in the shadows of the basement.

Sebastian was under Clemente's office window. Deliberately he set his shopping bag down, stooping to push it under a bush. He then crept forward, still in a crouch, his cane preceding him, until he was hidden by the foliage under the window. The bushes quivered and then were still.

Clemente had remarked that blind people's sense of touch was heightened, and I remembered reading that loss of sight had a similar effect on their hearing. Sebastian's keen ears had obviously picked up an interesting conversation in Clemente's office, something that made an excursion into the shrubbery worthwhile. Well, two could play.

I darted across the lawn and crept under the bushes at the far end of the window, trying to move as quietly as possible. The leaves rustled, and Sebastian started. I crouched, holding my breath. In seconds, he relaxed.

Clemente's voice came from within the rectory ". . . calm down, Jeff, and let's go over exactly what she said again."

"Again? She said she had *proof*, that's what!" Neverman's tone was agitated and high-pitched.

"But what kind of proof?" Clemente asked patiently.

"How should I know? She wouldn't tell me. All she said was she had proof, and if I didn't come back and live with her, she'd take it to the cops. She'll do it, too."

"You're being paranoid, Jeff. Take it easy and sit down. You've been pacing for ten minutes now. It won't help . . ." The peal of the telephone interrupted him. "Herb Clemente speaking."

In the short silence that followed, Neverman uttered an unintelligible curse. There was a thump, as if he had hit his fist against the wall.

"Look, take it a little slower," Clemente said

to the phone. "Who did this to you?"

A pause.

"No, wait! Don't hang up. I *do* care."

In moments, the receiver slammed down.

"Must be my day to be besieged by hysterical people," Clemente muttered.

"What?" Neverman asked distractedly.

"That was a girl I met last night. She's crying and carrying on, and I can't understand a word she says. So she accuses me of not caring about her, and hangs up."

Oh, my God! I thought. She's gotten worse again!

"Sounds like a wonderful little woman," Neverman said.

"Thing is, she's cute, and I'll bet a pretty good lay. But if she's that unstable, forget it."

I stiffened with anger at his shabby treatment of my friend and momentarily lost track of the conversation. I couldn't really blame Clemente for being wary of any involvement with Linnea, but I didn't want her hurt.

Clemente was saying, "How long did Anya give you to make up your mind?"

"She said I better show up there tonight, bag and baggage, or she'd go to the cops first thing tomorrow." He paused. "Maybe I could buy her off?" Neverman sounded slyly hopeful.

"Forget it, Jeff. No loan. Cash is tight right now, as you know. I'm making good on the fifty thousand tomorrow."

"So what do I do?"

"Well, Jeff." Clemente's voice held an undertone of amusement. "I see only one solution."

"What?"

"Pack your stuff, roll up your sleeping bag, and go home."

"Very funny."

"I mean it."

"There's got to be another way!"

Clemente replied, but evidently he had moved away from the window, for his words came out muffled.

"Goddamn it!" Neverman's voice rose. "*You* try living with her!"

"Fortunately I'm not the one she's crazy about. Now, I've wasted enough time on this problem. You'd better get your stuff together so you don't keep Anya waiting."

"Goddamned if I will! God*damned* if I will!" Neverman's voice escalated to a wail. "I'll see her dead before I'll live with her! Not you or the cops or anybody else can make me go back to her!"

The door slammed. I peered through the bushes at Neverman's departing back. He strode furiously toward the street, fists clenched at his sides.

Through the open window I heard Clemente mutter, "Jesus y Maria!"

I glanced at Sebastian. He relaxed his listening pose and crept from under the bushes, locating his shopping bag with his cane. I waited until he'd disappeared around the rectory before I emerged from hiding myself.

Neverman was far up the block on Twenty-fourth Street, crossing toward a small sidewalk cafe. Indifferent to traffic, he forced two cars to stop for him. A motorcycle roared around them, horn blaring, its driver shouting imprecations. Neverman gestured with his middle finger and kept on going. He entered the railed-off cafe and took a chair at a table with a red-and-white striped umbrella. I hurried up the street.

Neverman hunched over his table, drumming his fingers. I stopped in front of him, and he looked up with an anger-contorted face.

"Hi, Jeffrey," I said.

"What the hell are you doing? Following me? Herb told me you're a private cop. Did Anya hire you to keep tabs on me?"

"Of course not." I sat down uninvited. "Is something wrong?"

With an effort, he controlled his enraged expression. "Naw. I'm just getting some lunch. Can't take that swill at the Center any more."

I glanced at my watch.

"Three o'clock's late for lunch."

"I been busy. Didn't have time to eat before."

The weary-looking waitress came, and Neverman ordered a hamburger and fries. I asked for a Coke. When the food came, Neverman lubricated everything with catsup and dove in.

"So," he said, his mouth full, "you decide to take me up on my offer after all?"

"What offer?"

"Jesus!" He rolled his eyes exaggeratedly. "I

112

make a pass and you forget it What in hell did I ever see in you anyway?"

"You were pretty stoned last night."

"That must've been it."

"So the food at the Blind Center's bad?" I asked, to keep the conversation rolling.

"Yeah. You'd think they'd try to make it good. Those loonies over there don't have many other pleasures."

"Loonies like Sebastian, you mean."

He squeezed more catsup onto his plate. "Yeah, like Sebastian."

"What do you think of him, anyway?"

He glanced up briefly. "Like I said last night, he's like something out of the Addams Family. But most of them are. I guess if you can't see, you got a right to be crazy."

"Well, Herb Clemente is sane, at least," I said. "I hear you've known him a long time."

"Right," he said guardedly.

"Since he counseled you when you got out of prison."

He paused, hamburger halfway to his mouth. "Anya *did* tell you," he said flatly. "Herb wouldn't. It had to be her."

I shrugged. "What does it matter who told me?"

"Ah, that bitch. She can't keep her yap shut. Always got to tell people what rotten old Jeffrey did to her. 'Jeffrey went and got arrested on me. I waited for him all the time he was in jail, and then he left me. Rotten, horrible Jeffrey.' " Again, his harsh whine sounded remarkably like his wife.

"Do you blame her?" I asked.

"I blame *me* for getting mixed up with her in the first place."

"And for getting arrested?"

He heaved a sigh. "You sure are one-track. So I took a few things. Overloads. I'd short a customer now and then. Everybody does it. They've even got a name for it in the business — truckers' shortages. They expect it, it's built into their cost. Why should I be the one to get caught?"

"Just unlucky, I guess."

He shoved his plate away. "Look, Ms. Private Eye, don't sit there so smug. I took a fall for a lot of guys. Plenty of them were selling their overloads. We had regular setups with fences, regular prices. But who gets caught? Me. No trucking line would even hire me to sweep their loading dock now."

"Clemente hired you."

"Herb was upset that his counseling didn't work. I just can't get it together any more, and that's a blow to Herb's professional pride, so he took me in and made me his trained monkey. I got no illusions about Herb's reasons." Neverman stood up, pulling a couple of dollar bills from his jeans and tossing them on the table. One settled on his catsup-smeared plate. "Got to go." He turned and strode out of the cafe.

I rescued the bill from the pool of catsup and looked at the check. Neverman hadn't left enough to cover his meal. Sighing, I took the additional amount, plus the price of my Coke, from my bag. Call it a business expense, Sharon.

And now make it your business to find out more about the Sunrise Blind Center. There's something going on there that even your twenty-twenty vision can't see.

13

It was four o'clock when I returned to All Souls, where I could use the phone for free before business hours were over. I called the state Department of Health in Sacramento and, after being put on hold six times, finally reached the woman who had information on the Sunrise Blind Center.

My dear Uncle Jim, I explained — with mental apologies to that gentleman — had been blinded in an accident. His doctor had referred him to the Center. I had toured it and spoken with the director this afternoon, but I still had reservations. What could she tell me about the place?

Again on hold, I waited for her to fetch a file. I doubted I would learn anything revealing, but the possibility was worth the long-distance charge.

The woman came back on the line. Sunrise Blind Center had had an outstanding rehabilitation rate in the three years since its present director, Mr. Herbert Clemente, had taken over. The average period of time in which a resident returned to the community was less than a year. Both state and federal grants for the Center had recently been renewed.

And Mr. Clemente? I asked. What were his qualifications?

A rattling of paper. Mr. Clemente had a distinguished record of community service work. His B.A. in psychology was from California State University at Long Beach. He had served as a prison guard for five years, then run a halfway house for ex-convicts, and finally headed up a job-training and counseling program for parolees.

I wrote the word "parolees" on my legal pad and doodled a box around it as she talked. "The uncertainty of the length of time my Uncle Jim would have to remain at the Center disturbs me," I said stuffily when she had finished. "It's all well and good to speak of averages, but I know for a fact there's one man at the Center who's been in residence since Mr. Clemente became director."

A pause. "I don't have information on the individual patients, ma'am."

"Well, from your experience with this — and similar — programs, wouldn't you say that's an awfully long time?"

"Is the man severely handicapped?"

"Mr. Clemente described him as a very able worker."

"Perhaps, then, there's some problem that isn't readily observable. I suggest you take it up with Mr. Clemente."

I thanked her for the information and hung up.

"Parolees."

I stared down at the word, then went to Hank's office and stuck my head in the door.

"What's the name of your friend at the Department of Corrections?"

Hank looked up, owlish behind his thick glasses. "Dave Gardner. Why? What're you doing here? I thought you were investigating that murder."

"I am. Thanks."

Back in my office, I dialed the Department of Corrections and got Dave Gardner on the line. He'd done Hank many a favor in the past, and was glad to look up Jeffrey Neverman's record for me.

"It's not bad, as they go," he commented when he returned to the phone. "A couple of minor jail terms for D and D about ten years ago. Just brawls at a tavern over a waitress. Then the big one, grand theft. He drew three-to-five on that, was released two years ago September, and he's been a good boy ever since."

"What are the specifics on his offense?"

"He was caught ripping off merchandise from the truck line he drove for. It's a common practice, but the company decided to make an example of Neverman and prosecuted to the fullest. Your boy's just not lucky."

That was what Neverman thought too. I thanked Dave for his help, and he asked me to tell Hank he'd stop by sometime next week.

"I hope you'll be around the office, too," he added. "After all I've heard, I'd like to meet you."

What had Hank told him? Afraid to ask, I

merely said I'd like to meet him too.

Now for Sebastian. His long stay at the Blind Center puzzled me. Clemente had said the brush man had been blinded in an explosion at an oil refinery. There were a number of those dotting the shores of the Bay near Richmond and the Carquinez Straits, and a personnel department could tell me . . .

I stopped, chagrined. I didn't know Sebastian's last name.

Who would know? Who could I call without tipping off Clemente that I was prying into the Center's business?

I called the Albatross Superette. Mr. Moe answered, sounding rushed. Sebastian's last name was Hetzer. H-e-t-z-e-r. Why did I need to know?

"I have to write him a check for some brushes. Thanks." I hung up before he could ask why I didn't make it out to the Blind Center.

Fifteen minutes later, after only one wasted call, the personnel supervisor of Standard Oil in Point Richmond cautiously asked if he could call me back. I agreed, glad I had anticipated his precaution of ascertaining that All Souls Legal Cooperative really had a Ms. McCone who was checking Hetzer's references for possible employment under their program to hire the handicapped. I rushed down the hall to tip Ted that we momentarily had a personnel director and sat back to await the call.

Sebastian Hetzer had worked in maintenance

at the refinery since his discharge from the Army after Korea, the personnel man told me. The explosion and fire three years ago had been due to Hetzer's negligence, but the company had given him a settlement. He had immediately entered the burn-care unit of Letterman Army Hospital in San Francisco, and six months later had been referred to the Sunrise Blind Center.

What kind of worker was Hetzer?

Capable.

He did have a tendency to let personal problems interfere with his work. At the time of his accident, he'd been preoccupied with financial troubles.

"What kind of financial troubles?"

The personnel man chuckled. Hetzer liked to play the ponies. He often had to borrow to make up for his losses at Golden Gate Fields. It was a common failing.

What about future employment with Standard Oil? I asked. What if Hetzer should regain his sight?

A pause. "Obviously you haven't seen the man yet. His loss of sight was total, and there is no chance he could regain it. And, of course, he was very unpleasantly disfigured."

My calls completed, I cleared my desk and got ready to leave. The stories I'd gotten from Clemente, Neverman and Sebastian might check out, but there was one that didn't. It was what Mr. Moe had told me yesterday morning. I'd drive back home and confront him about it now.

At six-thirty, I arrived at the Albatross Superette. The store was empty once again, but I heard sounds out in the stockroom. I pushed the swinging door and looked in.

Mr. Moe stood with his back to me, lifting a squat green bottle from a carton. The harsh light of a bare bulb illuminated crates that held lettuce, oranges, and canned goods.

I knocked on the doorframe. "Mr. Moe, can I talk to you a minute?"

The grocer started, and he dropped the bottle. It smashed on the concrete floor. A puddle of liquid ran toward my feet, and I smelled the sharp odor of gin.

"I'm sorry I startled you!" I exclaimed.

Mr. Moe waved me away from the encroaching tide. "It is all right. But, please, it is dirty back here. Come out front. I will take care of this mess later." He shooed me into the store, latching the door of the stockroom.

"There was no difficulty about the check for Sebastian?" he asked. "The name I gave you was correct?"

"The check . . ." I'd almost forgotten the story I'd told him on the phone. "No, no difficulty."

"Good." He folded his arms across his chest and leaned against the counter. In spite of his polite expression, I sensed he was jumpy and anxious to be rid of me.

"Mr. Moe, I need to talk to you privately. Can you . . ." I gestured at the door.

"It is the dinner hour. I will lose customers if I close now." As if to emphasize his point, a man entered and asked for a carton of cigarettes. I waited while the grocer rang them up.

"All right, we can talk between customers," I said. "You see, I've discovered that you didn't tell me — or the police — the truth about the night before last."

He frowned elaborately. "I do not understand."

"I think you do. When I identified Molly's body, I saw her groceries on the floor, the groceries from this store."

"So you have said." Mr. Moe glanced nervously as a woman came in and headed for the produce aisle.

"There were eggs, oranges, and frozen lima beans." I paused. "The lima beans were still frozen. They had melted some, but not all that much."

Mr. Moe's eyes flickered and narrowed.

"You told me — and the police — that Molly bought those groceries around seven o'clock."

"That is true."

"No it isn't. I believed you, initially. It fit, almost exactly, with the established time of death."

The woman came out of the produce aisle with a head of lettuce. Mr. Moe rang it up, taking his time. When she had left, he turned to me. "I do not understand what is wrong, then."

"Molly could have come in here at seven and

returned home to surprise her killer — except for one thing."

"And that is?"

"The lima beans. They would have melted more if they'd been lying there on the floor since a little after seven."

He glanced at his watch. "Really, Miss McCone, I do not see what frozen vegetables have to do with this tragedy."

"Let me explain, then." I sat down on the wooden stool, smiling, as if this were a friendly visit.

His head moved toward the street entrance and then to the stockroom door. Obviously he was waiting for someone he didn't want me to see.

"The lima beans," I said, "should have melted more."

He frowned nervously. "Why?"

"Because I bought some here last night and tested how long it took them to defrost. In four hours, they were mushy, not firm like the ones in Molly's hall. Those had to have arrived at her apartment much later than you said."

Again, the agitated glance at his watch.

I pressed my advantage. "Well, Mr. Moe?"

"Perhaps I was mistaken about the time. It was a very busy night." He paused again and then added with growing conviction, "Yes, I am certain it was just before I closed, at ten."

A man came in. Mr. Moe jerked his head toward him, then relaxed. The man began looking over a rack of pipe tobacco.

I had the upper hand now. The grocer would tell me the truth, if only to be rid of me. "No, Mr. Moe. It couldn't have been. By the time you closed, Molly had been dead nearly two hours. The police have established that scientifically."

His mouth twitched. The man came up with a packet of tobacco and Mr. Moe rang it up, his hands shaking.

"Well?" I demanded.

He watched the man leave, then turned to me. What I could see of his eyes through the slits of his lids calculated rapidly. "All right, Miss McCone. I lied. I suppose you will report me to the police now."

"Not if you tell the truth this time."

He fingered the cash register keys. "That is fair. I will tell you. Mrs. Antonio called me with the grocery order. I often deliver to old ladies who are afraid to go out at night."

"When was this?"

"She called at seven o'clock. I did not lie about the time. I told her I would deliver the order after I closed and swept up."

"And you got there when?"

"Possibly ten thirty."

"How did you get in?"

"Someone had left the front door open, and also the door to Mrs. Antonio's apartment. At first, when she did not answer my knock, I thought she might have taken the garbage down or gone somewhere else in the building."

"And?"

He spread his hands, which trembled more now. "I went in, and she was lying on the floor. I do not remember crying out, but I set the groceries down by the telephone. I must have knocked them over. I do not remember anything more until I arrived home, upstairs." He motioned toward the ceiling. "All night I sat there in my front window. I saw Gus return from Ellen T's. I saw the police arrive. The ambulance leave. I sat and watched the empty street until morning, when I had to open the store."

"Did you see anyone else while you were in the building?"

"No."

"And you didn't touch anything at her apartment — search for anything?"

He frowned. "Of course not."

"Why didn't you tell the police?"

"I was afraid." He bowed his head. "Now I am ashamed."

"Afraid of what?"

"Miss McCone, you will not understand."

"Try me."

"You have no idea what it is to be an Arab in this city. There are many of us; for the most part we are in trade, with small shops and grocery stores. Every year many of us are robbed, and some are killed. The robbers are never caught, the killers never brought to justice. The police have no respect for us; they do not try to give protection. So we have contempt for the police — and fear."

It was true that Arab shopkeepers had been frequent targets of violence. Less prosperous ethnic groups within the city disliked and distrusted them. But Mr. Moe's paranoid little speech sounded strangely hollow. I watched him silently, wondering at his real reason for failing to report Molly's death.

Under my gaze, he shifted restlessly. "I have told you the truth. You will keep your part of the bargain?"

"Yes, I'll keep my part." I watched him a moment more, unable to gauge his truthfulness. Mr. Moe turned away.

"I have work to do now, Miss McCone. Please go."

I could have hung around outside to see who Mr. Moe was waiting for, but, in light of this new information, it seemed relatively unimportant. Instead, I went home — to check on Linnea's latest trauma.

14

When I opened the door to the apartment, the stereo blasted at me. Inside, I stepped on something and groped for the light switch. A box of chocolate creams had been overturned on the floor, a toilet brush incongruously lying among the candies. I stared in disgust at the gooey mess on my shoe.

"Oh Jesus," I muttered. The brush I had ordered from Sebastian the day before, but the chocolates could only mean Greg had been here. Had he questioned Linnea about the murder? Was that what had upset her?

I slipped out of my shoes and apprehensively went down the hall. The loud stereo meant my friend was drunk, at only seven in the evening.

She sat on the floor of the main room, cross-legged in front of the turntable. Her hair straggled from the childish braids, and a half-full fifth of Scotch stood on the floor beside her. The cat, terrified of the noise, cowered behind one of the chairs while Linnea swayed and cried to the Rolling Stones.

The Stones had been at the peak of their popularity during Linnea's courtship and early marriage. It didn't matter that their music wasn't particularly heart-wrenching. When Linnea sank into depression, she turned to their records, and to the bottle.

I went over and snapped the stereo off. Linnea raised her tear-streaked face. It was drawn into lines of suffering, but a self-satisfied light glowed in her eyes. I was taken aback: Was it possible she actually *enjoyed* her misery?

"Why're you doing that, for Christ's sake?" she demanded. Her tone was vague, and she glanced distractedly at the on-off switch.

I took a deep breath, telling myself: Don't let her make you feel guilty. This is not your fault.

"I turned it off because I want to talk to you. I can't do that with it on."

"Talk to me? That's just fine! *Now* you want to talk to me, after I've been calling and calling all day." She reached for the switch.

"Leave it off!" I spoke more sharply than I'd intended. Modulating my voice, I went on. "I'm sorry you couldn't reach me, but I've been busy. I'm free now, though, and we need to talk."

I sat down in one of the easy chairs, trying not to look too closely at the drink stains and cigarette burn on one arm. "Come over here so I don't have to shout."

She came, dragging the bottle and a smudged glass. She set them on the table between us and began to pour.

"No more Scotch, Linnea."

She looked up, eyes wide. "Christ, what is this? I need a drink, Sharon. I called you and left mes-

128

sages, but you didn't . . ."

"Listen, Linnea." Impatience wore my voice ragged. "I'm not your mother. Or your husband. Or some kind of keeper. I have a job to do, and I can't come running every time you get upset."

"Upset? You bet I'm upset!" Defiantly, she poured the Scotch. "What did you think you were doing, sending that guy over here to ask me questions?"

I thought of Greg's chocolate, and alarm flashed through me. "I didn't send him."

"Oh, sure you didn't! Oh, sure! It was a cute excuse, but I saw right through it." She gulped her drink. "He came in here like he owned the place. The creep!"

It *was* crummy of Greg to use the excuse of bringing chocolate to interrogate my friend! "What did he ask you?"

"Now you're interested, are you? After I called all day, now Ms. Big Shot Detective is interested."

I felt like slapping her, so I laced my fingers tightly together. "I asked, what did he want?"

My tone quelled her sarcasm. "He kept saying Molly had left something with me for safekeeping. He insisted I give it to him. But I didn't know what he was talking about. I told him I didn't, but he wouldn't believe me." Her voice descended to a childish whine. "Why wouldn't he believe me?"

"I don't know," I said absently. Why *did* Greg think Molly had left something with Linnea? Was

129

it possible she had secreted away some clue that would provide the answer to her death? After all, her apartment had been searched. I asked, "What happened then?"

"He kept on at me. I got scared. I took the chocolate and threw it at him. I screamed that I would call the cops. He just laughed at me."

I could imagine Greg's amusement. "And then?"

"He left. He just took off."

Fury bubbled up to replace my anxiety. This time Greg had gone one step too far. He had presumed on our friendship, counting on me not to file a complaint. Well, he'd soon learn differently.

"Okay, Linnea," I said. "It's over, and I'll see it doesn't happen again." Controlling my anger, I turned Greg's strange idea over in my mind. The something Molly had wanted kept safe must be a new lead. Greg had probably learned of Linnea's presence from one of the other tenants and — if he had also learned that Molly had been with her late on the day of the murder — he might have supposed Linnea was the one safe-guarding the mysterious object. But why the insistence when she denied it?

I believed her — because I thought I knew who the real guardian was.

I got up and reached for my bag.

"Where are you going?" Linnea demanded.

"Out. I have to see someone."

"After what I've been through, you're going

to leave me alone again?" Her hand hovered over her half-empty glass.

"As I explained before, I'm not your keeper. I have work to do. Why don't you take a nice, long bath and . . ."

"Some friend you are! It's just like when I called Herb, when I realized you weren't going to return my calls. He didn't even care about me. He said he didn't understand why I was so upset."

"Maybe he didn't understand what you were trying to tell him," I said, remembering the half of the phone conversation I'd overheard.

"Well, he should have! I needed him!"

"Lin, you can't always depend on other people. You have to take care of yourself."

"The hell you say! Oh, sure, you put on this big, independent act. That's only because you've never cared for anybody, and you never will!" Linnea reached for the bottle and began to pour. She missed the glass entirely, and Scotch ran all over the table, soaking a pile of magazines I hadn't had a chance to read yet.

The mess in the hall flashed before my eyes. I looked from the soaked magazines to a heap of clothing at the foot of the bed, and then to the cat, who still cowered behind the chair. With a sweeping gesture, I stepped forward, snatched the bottle, and hurled it against the opposite wall.

The bottle shattered. The cat shot under the bed. Liquor dribbled down to the baseboard.

Linnea's eyes grew wide, and her mouth opened soundlessly.

"Look, you bitch," I said in a low, furious voice, "I have absolutely had it with your whining and your crying. And your drinking. And your filthy habits."

"Sharon, I'm upset! My husband left me, and I don't have enough money, and . . ."

"Oh, Linnea, cut it out and grow up! Your problems aren't worth all this drama!"

"How can you say that? I've been through a tragedy!"

"Tragedy?" I exclaimed. "Look, Linnea, two nights ago I saw Molly lying up there with the life choked out of her. That's tragedy — not your petty little problems!"

She shrank back in the chair, lips parted.

"From now on, don't give me any more crap about how bad off you are and how lousy your life's turned out," I went on. "At least you've got life. If you want to throw it away, that's your business. But don't expect any more sympathy from me, because I've given you all I've got!"

I picked up my bag, put on another pair of shoes, and walked out.

In the lobby, I leaned my head against the wall, breathing hard. I hadn't done Linnea any good. She'd only reach for another bottle. And I hadn't done myself any good, either. All I'd done was lose my battle against the death of friendship.

A door slammed upstairs, and slow footsteps descended. Gus's voice spoke.

"Miss McCone! What's wrong?"

I faced the little gray man. "I had an argument with Linnea, that's all."

He nodded knowingly. "She drunk again?"

"Yes." I was too distraught to cover up for her.

Gus peered anxiously at my face. "You look terrible. Maybe you could use a drink yourself."

"I probably could."

"Look, why don't you go upstairs to my . . . to Molly's place? Sebastian's up there, and he'd enjoy the company. I've got to go to the funeral parlor to make the arrangements for Molly, and I'll be gone an hour or two."

"Are you sure he wouldn't mind?"

"Positive."

"I'll do it then." I gave his arm a grateful squeeze and started upstairs.

Sebastian's voice answered my knock. The door was unlatched, and I let myself in. I would have been more careful in an apartment where a murder had recently taken place, but maybe the brush man subscribed to the theory of the already-stolen horse. He certainly seemed relaxed, in Molly's favorite chair, listening to classical music on her FM.

I explained why I was there, and Sebastian nodded sympathetically. "There's a bottle of brandy in the kitchen. Help yourself. And get me a little more while you're at it, would you?"

The glass he held out was one of Molly's best crystal set. As I poured the liquor — an excellent brand that she probably had been saving for a special occasion — I reflected that Gus and Sebastian had slipped into a very confident attitude of possession toward Molly's things. When I returned to the living room, I said, a little bitchily:

"Well, you two seem all settled in."

A smile distorted Sebastian's scarred face. "Gus invited me for dinner — Kentucky Fried Chicken. Somebody's gonna have to teach him to cook. Anyway, I said I'd wait here until he got back from the undertaker, to save him the trip to the Center until afterwards."

I was glad he couldn't see the dubious look on my face. I sat down on the couch and asked, "How's Gus holding up?"

"As well as you could expect. He moped around here all day, and I was surprised he didn't want me to go along to the undertaker, but he said he should do it alone."

"You haven't been working, then."

"No, but we got to make rounds tomorrow. The racks'll be getting low, and Mr. Clemente hates to have them that way."

"Speaking of him, he gave me a tour of the Center today. I hung around there for a while afterwards. You should really be more careful who's watching when you eavesdrop."

His lips quivered. "You saw me, in the bushes?"

"I sure did."

"Was anybody else there?"

"Nope. Your guilty secret is safe with me. What was going on in Clemente's office?"

Nervously, he stroked the front of his yellow

sweater. "Just a bunch of talk about Neverman's woman problems."

"It must have been interesting; you listened long enough."

"Miss McCone, let me explain. I kind of like to keep an ear to the ground at the Center. You never know what's happening there, and I was worried about whether the new grants had been approved. When it's the only home you've got, you like to know what's going on, but nobody ever tells us anything."

"Well, just don't get caught."

"I never figured anybody would see me in a place where almost everybody's blind. I'll take more care in the future."

Sebastian continued to stroke his sweater. It looked like cashmere, silky and soft to the touch. I recalled that he had another like it, a red one. To a blind person, tactile pleasure was important, but it seemed an expensive way to enjoy oneself. The oil company personnel man had commented on Sebastian's fondness for betting on horses. Perhaps that was now transformed into a liking for luxury.

I asked, "How come you still live at the Center, Sebastian? Herb tells me you were there when he arrived, and most residents leave within a year of being admitted."

"I came a little after Mr. Clemente did. The reason I stay is I've got no place to go. Most of the others have resources or family, but I'm alone in the world."

"You don't have any money? Surely your former company must have made you some sort of settlement."

"They did." He sipped his brandy, licking his lips appreciatively. "Sixty thousand dollars worth. It was a nice nest-egg, but some of it I spent and the rest I made a bad investment with. I lost it all. Never was very lucky with money."

"What kind of investment?"

"Oh, one of those get-rich-quick schemes. I don't want to talk about it. It depresses me."

He'd probably invested in Arizona desert land or a Ponzi scheme. I finished my brandy. It was time I got on with my search for whatever Molly had hidden away.

"Thanks for the drink, Sebastian," I said. "I have to be going now."

"So soon?"

"Duty calls."

"You working tonight?"

"Yes."

"You're an ambitious young lady."

But it wasn't ambition that drove me right now. It was curiosity, coupled with a strong desire to see justice done.

15

Madame Anya answered my knock quickly, her eager, flushed face a contrast to the gun in her hand. At the sight of me, she shrank back in disappointment. It was several seconds before she recovered herself and put on a polite, professional smile.

"Good. You've come about the candles."

"No. I need to talk to you about Molly."

"Now? So late?"

I looked at my watch. "It's not yet nine."

"Isn't it? Somehow it seems so much later."

It always did, if you were waiting for someone as I suspected Anya was for Jeffrey. "Please — this is important."

She sighed heavily. "All right, but first let me put Hugo in his cage." She turned, slipping the gun into the table drawer as she had last night, and shut the door briefly before admitting me.

The room was unchanged. The bird statues held their various poses: singing, cocking their little heads, roosting on wax nests. Anya herself was different, however. Clad in a long black dress and fringed silk shawl of red and gold poppies, she looked every bit her role of prophetess. Her hair was swept up on her head by an ornate silver comb, and her lips shone with crimson gloss. I wondered if she had dressed up for Jeffrey's return — and if indeed there would be one.

She motioned me into a chair and asked with a touch of impatience, "Well, what is it, honey?"

"Anya, you and Molly were good friends, right?"

"The best."

"She confided in you?"

"Naturally. She came to me for spiritual advice every week. She held nothing back."

"And, since you were such good friends, you want to see her killer caught, don't you?"

She frowned. "Of course. I don't see what you're getting at."

"Just this: The day she was killed, Molly came to you for her weekly consultation. I'm sure she told you about the things that were bothering her. What she said could lead me to her killer."

Anya drew the shawl more closely around her shoulders. "You're asking me to betray a professional confidence, honey. I told you last night, I can't do that. It's like asking a doctor to show you a patient's case history. Or asking a lawyer what his client said to him in private."

The overly grand comparisons irritated me, but I said, "It's permissible to give out that kind of information to aid in a murder investigation. Even psychiatrists will do that."

She sat up straighter. "I suppose you're right. We professionals do have a duty . . ." A sudden thought seemed to hit her. "Wait, are you investigating the murder? For All Souls?"

"How do you know where I work?"

"From Molly. She often told me useful things
. . ." Again she paused, flushing.

"Like the things about my friend Linnea that
you probably used in her reading. And the things
you used in mine last night."

"We meant no harm. You've got to understand."

"Understand what?"

"It's hard to make a living in this business,
honey. A little inside information makes the reading more convincing."

"Look, I'm not here to question your ethics.
I want to know what Molly told you."

She was silent.

"Whatever it was, it's been extremely useful
to you."

"I don't know what you mean." She tried to
feign indignance, but the words came out flat.

"Yes, you do, Anya. Molly told you something,
something that's given you power over Jeffrey
again. You'd been looking for that leverage for
a long time."

Stubbornly she shook her head.

"Do you deny you called Jeffrey at the Blind
Center around eleven last night?"

"I didn't!"

"I was there, Anya."

"Well, doesn't a wife have the right to call
her husband? I needed to ask him some questions
about . . . about our joint income tax return."

139

"Whatever you said, I don't think you went into your real business on the phone. You probably made an appointment with him — I'd say for early this afternoon."

Her dark eyes glittered. "Why would I do that?"

"To issue an ultimatum. To tell him either he come home to you or you would go to the police with the thing Molly left with you for safekeeping. Whatever that thing is, it implicates Jeffrey in her death, doesn't it?"

"No!" she exclaimed. "No! It certainly does not!"

"Then at least you admit Molly left something with you. What was it? Was it the thing Jeffrey couldn't find when he searched her apartment the other night?"

"He didn't!"

"Do you really want to coerce a murderer into living with you? Doesn't that seem awfully risky?"

Anya bent her head. "He's not a murderer," she whispered.

Cruelly, I pressed on. "Oh, no? Do you know what Jeffrey told Herb Clemente this afternoon? He said he'd rather see you dead than come back to you. That doesn't sound like a man I'd want in *my* house."

Her head came up, and her mouth formed a little "o" before her hand covered it.

Sickened by the way I'd demolished her world, I forced myself to continue. "It's true, Anya. I heard him."

The crow moved restively in its cage. After a long moment, Anya lowered her hand and asked weakly, "He's not coming home, is he?"

"No, he's not. He doesn't love you, and you're better off without him. Now will you give me whatever Molly . . ."

"No!" She jumped to her feet, fists clenched in sudden panic. Frantically she turned this way and that, as if she were cornered. The gay scarf slipped from her shoulders to the floor, where she trampled it.

"I won't let you do this to me!" she wailed. "You can't spoil Jeffrey's homecoming! Why, I dressed up for him. I made him a cake. I bought his favorite whiskey. He's got to come. He will. You'll see."

Her breath came in pants, and her glistening eyes darted desperately from side to side. I had the frightening sensation that something deep inside of her had snapped. Suddenly she whirled on me, her face alight with insane hope.

"Look, I can prove it," she announced. "I can prove he's not a killer. I have something to show you. Go look, please." She stretched out a shaking hand toward the archway at the rear of the room.

I went where she pointed. It was a closed door off the hallway.

"Open it," Anya commanded from behind me.

It was an ordinary bathroom. "I don't see what . . ."

As I turned, Anya came on in a rush. She pushed me into the room, and my hip slammed into the washbasin. The door began to close. I lunged for it, then shrank back. Anya thrust the crow inside.

In horror, I retreated to the far end of the narrow room. The crow flapped about, looking for a place to light. Brushing me with frantic wings, it landed on the shower curtain rod. There it perched, screeching in distress.

I cringed against the wall, breathing hard.

Aloud, I said, "Sharon, it's a ridiculous fear! Calm down. Don't scare the thing. It might fly again."

The crow was between me and the door. I looked for another exit. There was a window to my left, but it was nailed shut. Even if I got it open, I was three stories above the ground. Still . . .

My eye on the crow, I rummaged in my bag for a suitable implement. All I found was a corkscrew. It would have to do. I sidled over to the window and began to pry at the nails.

The crow took off. Its wings flapped wildly. I almost dropped the corkscrew. The bird landed on top of the medicine chest and screeched louder.

I watched it for a minute, aware of voices in the hall beyond the closed door. Anya had called in reinforcements. My palms felt clammy as I turned back to the window. The nails began to yield.

After what seemed like hours of feverish work, the nails gave way. I thrust the window open and crouched down, covering my head with my arms.

"Come on, Hugo. Nice Hugo," I coaxed. "See the open window? There's all that world outside."

The bird ceased screeching. I hazarded a look. His head was cocked in curiosity. In seconds, he flapped over and perched on the sill. I crawled toward the door.

The bird's head bobbed from side to side. Then his wings spread, and he was gone.

I stood up and looked for a weapon. The light metal towel rack was the kind that snapped onto brackets. I popped it off and hefted it. It was scarcely heavy enough to swat a fly, but, like the corkscrew, it would have to do.

Cautiously, I turned the knob and opened the door a crack. All was quiet. I opened it further. No voices. The towel bar upraised, I stepped into the hall and crept along to the archway.

Anya lay crumpled on the living room floor, like a rag doll a child had discarded after play.

I staggered and dropped the towel bar, then leaned in the archway, staring at her prone figure.

"This is too much," I said aloud. "Two people killed in two days. It's too much."

No, maybe she's not dead. Go over and see if she's dead.

"I can't. I can't take any more."

Goon. You've got to.

"I can't!"

Go!

I knelt beside her, pushing back her hair where it had come loose from the comb and fallen over her face. Her blood-suffused eyes stared sightlessly. Her face was a mottled purple. The bruises on her throat told me all I needed to know.

I got up and backed away, stumbling over a chair. How long had I been imprisoned in the bathroom? Ten minutes? Fifteen? How long since I'd heard the voices? I'd lost all sense of time. I'd been so preoccupied with the goddamned bird that I hadn't noticed a thing.

It was important to stay cool now and figure out if the killer had gotten what Anya had been holding for Molly. Where would she have hidden it?

People hid things in strange and unsuitable places. Money in the mattress, marijuana in the Band-Aid box, jewelry in the cookie jar.

I began to search.

Anya had several dozen boxes of bird charms, like the ones she'd given Linnea and me, in the linen closet. The bathroom cabinet held enough toilet paper to supply a small army. She kept candy in the bedside table, extra handkerchiefs stuffed down beside the cushion of her chair, and an unusual number of her books were shelved upside down.

I moved stealthily, using pieces of Kleenex to avoid leaving fingerprints.

In the kitchen, I found the chocolate cake Anya had baked for Jeffrey. A bottle of Wild Turkey stood on the table beside it. Delicate plates, cut-crystal glasses, and silver forks had been laid out.

What a pathetic fantasy the fortune teller had been enacting! After blackmailing Jeffrey into coming home, she had supposed they would have a festive little party and live happily ever after. I felt a rush of pity for her.

Anya's cupboards were well-stocked with staples and cereals and canned goods. A few dishes stood clean in the drainer. Her appliances sparkled. The refrigerator contained milk and fresh vegetables and a bottle of good wine. The freezer held meat and TV dinners and a box of nylons.

Elated, I snatched it from the cold depths. There were three pair of a standard brand of knee-high stockings designed to be worn with pants.

This had to be it. But what on earth could it mean?

The telephone rang, shattering both the silence and my nerves. I stared at it, paralyzed, then jammed the nylons in my bag. I'd better get out of here fast. Hopefully I wouldn't run into anyone on the stairs.

At Anya's front door, however, I stopped. The drawer of the little table beside it was open. And empty. The killer had taken the fortune teller's gun.

I went out and hurried downstairs, past my apartment, where the stereo once more blared. I'd report the murder anonymously from the phone booth on the corner, then be on my way. I should stick around, but I didn't want to waste precious time explaining to the police what I was doing in the bathroom with a bird while Anya was getting murdered.

16

When I stepped out of the phone booth, the blue Blind Center van pulled up to the Albatross Superette. Neverman was at the wheel.

Just the man I wanted to see.

Mr. Moe came out of the store and fumbled with a set of keys. Neverman's hand beat an impatient rhythm on the steering wheel.

I ran to where I'd parked my car before talking with Mr. Moe. Getting in, I twisted the rearview mirror until it showed the grocer climb into the van.

Neverman backed up, made a sweeping U-turn in the intersection, and drove past my parking space, headed south on Guerrero. I started up and followed.

At Army Street, the van turned left and led me toward the freeway. It went past the cluttered hump of Bernal Heights and swept under the interchange, ignoring the on-ramps. I tailed it along Army, deep into the industrial sector of the city, pulling back as traffic lightened.

At Third Street, the last major artery before the Bay, the van turned again. Here the traffic was nonexistent, and I had to drop back further. We were headed for the area known as India

Basin, next to the old Hunters Point Naval Shipyard.

In spite of the distance I had to maintain, the taillights of the van were easy to spot. They disappeared to the left as the clumsy shapes of World War II housing on the hill above the shipyard came into view. I speeded up and cruised by in time to see the van drive down a lane between two gas storage tanks.

I backed up and followed the lane to a dilapidated cyclone fence. My headlights picked out a brick guard post with smashed windows. Blackberry vines and weeds had taken over here, snaking up the walls of the little gatehouse and twining in the lattices of the fence. A sign leaned at a crazy angle among them, as if it had fallen there:

SAN FRANCISCO IRON WORKS, INDIA BASIN DIVISION

PRIVATE PROPERTY — NO TRESPASSING

The gate sagged open on broken hinges. Beyond it, a narrow road led between hulking factory buildings. Not a light showed. The van was nowhere in sight.

Quickly I pulled behind the guardhouse and cut off my motor. I unlocked the glovebox and took out my gun, slipping it into an outer compartment of my shoulderbag that acted as a holster.

The road on the other side of the fence was

full of potholes. I walked far to one side, next to the wall of the factory. The buildings were ponderous brick structures with huge arching windows and doors. What moonlight filtered down into the chasm between them picked out jagged holes in the many-paned glass. Occasionally my feet crunched on shards of it as I made my way toward the open space at the other end.

There I paused. The moonlight provided better visibility here. It outlined heaps of rubble dotting a flat plain that ended at the shore of the Bay. A tortured wreck of a corrugated-iron building stretched its twisted beams toward the sky. From far to my left I heard a rhythmic clanking.

I peered around the building in the direction of the sound. The van was moving slowly onto a pier with a large warehouse at the end. The headlights bumped up and down with each clank. The pier must be an old one, resurfaced with metal slabs that had come loose.

Afraid to cross the open space where moonlight created a murky dusk, I kept to the wall of the old factory until I had no choice but to sprint toward the pier. There I hid behind an upright post. The van had stopped midway between me and the warehouse.

Mr. Moe's slender figure emerged from the passenger side. He leaned back in, conferring with Neverman, then approached the warehouse. The lights of the van went out.

I slipped forward to the next post.

A small door in the warehouse opened. For an instant, a burly man was silhouetted against the light inside. He beckoned to Mr. Moe. The grocer entered, and the door shut. No light leaked from around its frame.

I kept creeping forward.

The faint orange tip of a cigarette glowed inside the van. Neverman's head was outlined against the waters of the Bay. He had the radio tuned to a country and western station, and the monotonous thump of the guitars blended with the sloshing of the waves under the pier.

When I reached the post closest to the van, a sudden breeze brought me the acrid odor of marijuana smoke. It was a startling intrusion upon the smells of tar, creosote, and stagnant sea water. I crouched behind the post, debating what to do next.

Neverman was obviously not at his most alert. Should I chance taking him by surprise?

No way, I decided. I didn't know how many others were inside that warehouse.

Or what they were doing.

Or why Neverman hadn't gone inside with Mr. Moe.

Restlessly, I moved my foot. It hit something light that tipped over and rolled onto the metal surface toward the center of the pier. It rattled along, making an incredible racket for what could be only a pop or beer can. I shrank back against the post, hoping Neverman was too stoned to notice.

"Who's there?" His shout echoed up and down the pier.

I turned and ran.

"Hey! Come back here!"

My feet clanked along the metal slabs. I stumbled when I hit flat ground.

"Stop, you!"

Neverman's footsteps staggered down the pier. I dived behind a pile of bricks.

The warehouse door clanged open.

"What the hell's going on out here?" a rough voice shouted.

I dodged from one heap of bricks to another, toward the ruined building I'd seen earlier.

"Neverman! Hold it!" Mr. Moe's voice rang out.

I crawled into the half-demolished building on my hands and knees. Pieces of glass and metal cut into me. My pants ripped with a sickening sound.

I lay flat on the ground, under a tilted piece of corrugated iron, my gun out, waiting for them. My cheek pressed into the rubble, and I sucked in grit with every ragged breath.

Miraculously, no one came.

After a few minutes, I inched forward and hazarded a look. Four figures stood at the foot of the pier. Neverman and Mr. Moe and two larger men. They milled about, then walked back toward the warehouse. Mr. Moe and Neverman parted company with the others at the van. It started and backed down the pier, then bumped across the debris-filled field toward the old factory and the gate.

Obviously they didn't want to attract attention by using their headlights to search for me.

I lay still, listening to the silence. From far off, a ship's horn groaned. The faint bellow of foghorns answered it. I wouldn't be surprised if we had rain by morning.

After a while, I crawled from under the piece of iron. My clothes were a mess, and my rear end was definitely open to the night air. I slipped from rubbish heap to rubbish heap and plunged into the alley between the two factory buildings. In their ponderous silence they took on an evil, Dickensian air. I hurried along to my car.

It was where I'd left it, untouched and apparently unobserved. I started up and pulled away with a spray of gravel. After an adventure like this, the best place for me was home in bed. Given Linnea's condition, however, that wasn't possible. I'd have to settle for my office at All Souls.

17

I was in my office, sewing up the rip in the seat of my pants, when Hank barged in. He scratched furiously at his head and muttered, "Oh, you're not dressed."

"No, I'm not." I draped the pants over my bare legs. "Why don't you come back in about five minutes."

"Uh, sure." He backed out the door, his eyes bemused as he tried to act as if finding me half-naked in my office were an everyday event.

I chuckled softly while I inspected my repair job. The pants were intact, but they would never be the same. As I was putting them on, Hank knocked and, after an elaborate pause, re-entered. His tall, lanky frame seemed to fill the little room.

"Ted mentioned you'd snuck in the back way, holding yourself together," he said, perching on the edge of my desk. "I thought I'd better check things out."

I'd parked two blocks away and slipped down the stone footpath that scaled the hill behind All Souls, hoping no one would see me. Ted, the paralegal worker and receptionist, had been fixing a snack in the kitchen when I'd come through the service porch, and he'd made appropriately lewd comments.

"Well, I'm *sewn* together now." I sat down in my ratty armchair.

Hank grinned. "You're having a rough vacation. Exactly how did you split your britches?"

"It would take years in the telling."

"I've got all night. Besides, I don't think it would be smart for you to leave here."

"Oh?"

"Our friend Greg Marcus was here — minus his usual candy bar. Seems you're wanted for questioning in a homicide."

"Oh, Lord. I was afraid of that. How'd he figure out I reported it?"

"For one thing, the murder was in your building — again. For another, a young-sounding woman reported it. And, when Greg went looking for you, you were missing from your usual haunts."

"That's pretty flimsy evidence to put out a warrant on."

"I don't think there's a warrant yet. He said something about keeping it friendly. But he's got better evidence than what I just told you."

"What?"

"Greg went to your apartment. Your houseguest answered the door, drunk as a skunk."

"Oh, God."

"When Greg asked where you were, your friend said she didn't know, that you might have paid another visit to 'that goddamned fortune teller' far as she knew."

"Oh, Linnea!" I wailed.

"She sounds like a delightful guest."

"She's getting more so every day. Hank, do you think Greg will come back here tonight?"

"Nope. He thinks you're too clever to show your face in these parts. If you stay inside, you're safe. So how about telling me how you ripped your pants?"

"Why? So you can go back and gossip with Ted?"

"Now," Hank admonished, "you know we're only interested in your welfare. I came right down here to reassure myself . . ."

"You mean to get the dirt. It's no wonder it's impossible to maintain one's dignity around this place!"

"Aw, Shar, aren't you going to let me in on it?"

The teasing light in his eyes was infectious. "What's it worth to you?"

He considered. "A damned good cup of coffee. I brewed some of that French roast you like a while ago."

"It's a deal. Let me clean up and brush my hair first."

"I'll go wash some cups."

When I went into the kitchen, Hank sat at the big table, two steaming mugs and a bottle of brandy in front of him. "Didn't think you'd mind." He motioned at the bottle. "Makes for better storytelling."

I thought back to the brandy I'd shared with

Sebastian. It seemed like years ago. "Mind? Not in the slightest."

"So tell me your strange and wonderful tale," Hank commanded.

I told all of it, not even bothering to edit the scene at Anya's. When I got to the part about being imprisoned in the bathroom with the bird, Hank stroked his chin, pulling at the corners of his mouth to keep them from turning up. When I was finished, he looked more serious.

"What do you think Anya planned to do with you?" he asked.

"I don't know. She knew I was afraid of birds, but not that it was a serious phobia. Actually, I think she just flipped out."

"And you heard voices while you were trapped in the john?"

"Yes. I thought she'd called someone in to help her. I still think whoever it was must have been someone she knew."

"Why so?"

"Because Anya had a habit of answering her door with a gun. She must have put it away and let this person in. Then, after he killed her, he took the gun from the table drawer."

"You sound like you think it might not have been the husband."

"Everything points to him, though. Even though I saw him pick up Mr. Moe right after I called the cops, he still had plenty of time to go back to the Blind Center and get the truck. I must have searched Anya's apartment for a good fifteen minutes before I made that call."

"And what was it you found? Nylons?"

"Yes. Wait a minute." I hurried back to my office and got the box of nylons from my bag. Returning to the kitchen, I tossed it on the table.

" 'Knee-Hi's,' " Hank read. "What is this?"

"Something that makes no sense whatsoever. But they have to be what Molly gave Anya; I found them in the freezer."

"That still doesn't explain about your pants."

"I'm getting to that." I went on with my narrative.

"You've had a busy evening," Hank commented when I'd finished. He poured us more coffee and brandy. "So what does it all mean?"

"I'm not sure." I turned the box of nylons over in my hands, then opened it and dumped the plastic packets out on the table.

"What're these?" Hank picked up two IBM-type cards that had fallen out with them.

"Let me see." I snatched one from his fingers.

"God, you're grabby. You recognize it?"

"Sort of. This, my friend, is a stock-control card. I remember them well from my department store days." I read aloud from the card. " 'System-a-Tron, a Retail Management Plan.' "

"Oh, one of those cards that goes in with the merchandise," Hank said. "When the salesclerk gets to it, she forwards it to the computer, and it tells the computer it's time to reorder."

"Plus provides statistics on sales volume and

156

turnover." I looked at the figures printed in the boxes on top of the card. "These nylons are Stock Number 40/KB-1216 in Department Number CN43 of the Knudsen Department Store. . . ."

"What's wrong?"

"Hush." I held up a hand. "It's starting to fit."

Hank drained his coffee cup, watching me silently.

"Okay," I said after a minute, "I think I've got it. I'll take it slow, from the beginning."

"All right."

"Start with the Blind Center. The other day, Sebastian offered to sell me some shoelaces. He said they had expanded their line to products they didn't manufacture, products they bought wholesale. But when I mentioned it to Herb Clemente, he got upset. He indicated Sebastian wasn't supposed to sell those items yet. My impression was that Sebastian had taken the stuff and pocketed what he made on it."

"Taken it from where?"

"The basement of the church at the Center. They've got a whole storeroom of stuff like dishwashing gloves and wooden spoons and other kitchen equipment. Lord knows what else they've got in there; I didn't take time to explore it completely."

"So what do they plan to do with it?"

"Clemente said they were going to sell it as soon as they got new racks to hold that type of thing."

157

"And you think that's strange?"

"Wait, I'm not through. This Jeffrey Neverman used to be a trucker. Like I told you, he went to prison for ripping off his employer. It's a common enough crime — I remember how, when I worked in security, truckers would take an extra case or two of merchandise from the loading dock or short a customer at the other end. The kinds of things the Blind Center has in that storeroom are the sort that are pilfered all the time."

"Ahah!" Hank exclaimed. "So you think the Center is buying stolen goods?"

"Yes, probably through Neverman's contacts among truckers."

"Where do these nylons fit in?"

"The stock cards tell me they were stolen, probably from Knudsen's warehouse after they'd been readied to go on the selling floor. I can't prove it, but I think Molly bought them off of Sebastian. Molly used to work at Knudsen's, and she would have recognized their cards and known what they meant."

Hank scratched his head. "All right, you knew this Molly person. What do you think she would have done about it?"

"First, I think she'd have consulted Anya Neverman, whom she considered a spiritual advisor. In fact, finding these nylons in Anya's freezer makes me sure that's what she did. Anya probably proposed several solutions: Keep shut up about it, complain to Clemente, or go to the cops. She probably advised against the latter, not wanting Jeffrey to go to jail again. Molly also had a genuine concern in the matter, since her husband leads Sebastian on his rounds. She was a very righteous woman, and I don't think she'd want Gus involved in a crime."

"So, of the other two alternatives, which did she take?"

I ignored the question. "None of the alternatives was pleasant to her. She told Linnea that Anya hadn't offered any solution that wouldn't make her problem worse. She also said she wished she'd never seen the cards. Both Linnea and I took that to mean Tarot cards, but she was actually talking about these." I waved the IBM-type cards.

"But which alternative *did* she take?"

"I think she complained to Clemente. She may have told him she had proof stashed with someone in the building. She'd left the nylons with Anya, just to be on the safe side."

"And Clemente killed her?"

"I don't know about Clemente. He's just a dis-illusioned liberal. Neverman, maybe. Possibly Mr. Moe. He's involved in this, in some peripheral way, and I have only his word that he found the body and was so shaken he ran."

"And tonight someone killed Anya because she also knew about the scheme?"

"Yes. No one would have realized she did, except for her passion for Jeffrey. She gave herself away when she tried to blackmail him into coming home."

Hank tipped the coffeepot, but only a few drops

trickled out. "It's gone. You want straight brandy?"

"Sure. Why not?"

He poured it. I sipped absently.

"So where are we now?" Hank asked. "Do you tip the police to what's going on at the Center?"

"It wouldn't do any good."

"Why not, if they've got a whole storeroom full of stolen goods?"

"In security, I learned a good bit about the way fences operate. Any smart fence covers himself with bogus receipts. They have bookkeeping systems and cancelled checks to show they bought and paid for the stuff. Even if the supposed seller is on the shady side, they can claim they didn't know the stuff was stolen."

Hank nodded. "The way the law reads, in order to convict of receiving, you have to prove that the stuff was stolen, that it was in the accused's possession, and that the accused was aware it was stolen. That last is the toughest to do."

"And Clemente's a smart man, so you can be sure he's covered himself completely."

"What I wonder," Hank said, "is why they're going to risk selling hot goods on the Center's racks."

"I doubt they are. Clemente may have just said that. The Center is probably a way station for the goods en route to the final purchaser — a drop, it's called. But what a place for a drop!" I laughed.

"What's so funny?"

"If you wanted to store stuff where nobody would see it, what better place than a blind center?"

Hank chuckled.

"And it explains why they haven't fixed that burnt-out roof," I added. "They really don't want the workshop in there, because it would mean having more people — maybe sighted visitors — around."

I leaned my chin on my hands, staring out the kitchen window at the lights of downtown. They had been winking off steadily; it was after two in the morning. My head was beginning to whirl — either from the excitement or the brandy.

Hank, however, never got tired. "What about the people out at the old iron works?" he asked. "Who were they?"

"Thieves, probably. Moe and Neverman were most likely arranging a drop."

"I read something about rip-offs just last weekend," Hank said. "Let me see if I can find it." He hurried off to his office.

I sighed wearily. Hank was an information freak. His office was papered with maps of every type and description. He saved his *National Geographic*s for years. He subscribed to the *New York Times*, *Washington Post*, and *Wall Street Journal*, as well as the local papers. Often he stacked back issues in great piles all over his office. With a sense more accurate than radar, he always knew how to put his hands on a particular clipping. If he got started now, we'd be up all night.

He bustled back into the kitchen, brandishing a section of the *San Francisco Chronicle*. "It's a backgrounder for a news item on the theft of two containers of Tanqueray gin from Circle Wharf and Warehouse in Alameda last Thursday," he announced. "Seems like somebody made off with two forty-foot containerized shipments of the stuff, worth around four hundred and sixty thousand dollars."

He riffled through the pages of the paper. "Anyhow, what's interesting is the statistics on cargo pilferage in the background story. Listen to this: for the ports of San Francisco, Oakland, and Alameda, and the two airports, cargo pilferage amounted to $194,966 last year alone — and they say that figure is only eighty percent accurate. Wow, that latest theft is really going to boost this year's figure!"

Wide awake and bright-eyed, Hank pored over the article, picking out statistics with his forefinger. "Catch this quote, will you! 'Any veteran of the waterfront will tell you he doesn't take anything, but he has plenty of coworkers who consider pilfering little more than a fringe benefit.' "

I yawned. "That's how Neverman described it."

"They say it's hard to locate the weak link in the security chain — it can be in the freight station itself, after cargo clears Customs, with the truckers, or at the consignee's own warehouse after the merchandise is accepted."

I yawned again.

"Circle Wharf and Warehouse also recently lost fifty-one bags of Colombian coffee worth twenty thousand dollars. That much for only fifty-one bags! No wonder it's so expensive. Corned beef is another item that's pilfered a lot. I wonder why. . . ." He paused, frowning at me. "Am I keeping you up?"

"As a matter of fact, I wonder if I could sleep on the couch tonight?"

He grinned. "Sorry. I do have a tendency to ramble on into the wee hours. I'll get you some blankets."

I cleared the coffee mugs and, when Hank delivered the bedding, curled up on the long leather sofa in the combination living-and-waiting room. My head still spun. It definitely must be the brandy, I decided, as I fell into a deep sleep.

18

I awakened the next morning to a big brown eye staring unblinkingly into mine. Soft little breaths tickled my face.

A voice spoke in Chinese, and the eye disappeared. I jerked upright and saw a small girl scamper across the room to where her mother sat knitting. She scolded the child and pulled her into the chair beside her.

I shrank back down and looked at my watch. Almost ten o'clock. What were they doing, letting me oversleep in the waiting room with the clients!

Hastily, I got up and gathered the blankets. "Rough night — busy litigating," I muttered as I backed out the door.

Halfway down the hall, I bumped into Hank. He had my bag and jacket in hand. "Here, take these. Give me those blankets," he commanded.

"What? What's . . ."

"Greg's out front. Ted's stalling him. You'd better get out of here, if you don't want to wind up your investigation in a cell."

"Oh, Lord! Thanks. I . . ."

"Go!"

I crashed through the waiting room and the kitchen to the service porch. As I went out the back gate and climbed the hill, I wondered what the client with the little girl had thought. If she'd been there before, she was probably used to all sorts of strange behavior.

The stone steps were slippery with fine, gray rain, a rarity for the month of June. When I reached my MG, I ran the defroster for a few minutes. My face looked pasty in the rearview mirror, and my hair was tangled and snarled. I brushed it, which helped some. I could still do with a toothbrush, a bath, and a change of clothes. A couple of aspirin wouldn't hurt either.

So Greg was anxious to locate me. That meant he probably had a man on my apartment. The last thing I needed this morning was to unravel my complicated discovery for Greg, and lose time explaining why I'd fled the scene of a crime, an offense for which I could lose my license. The only way out of this jam was to find the killer and present him to Greg like a box of See's candy.

I drove to Guerrero Street, cursing the wiper blades that never got the windshield clear. Sure enough, a vehicle with the unmistakable aura of unmarked cop car stood at my curb. Head averted, I went on to the intersection.

The Superette was a hive of activity. Trucks from the Produce Terminal, the bakeries, and the grocery wholesalers double parked, unloading crates onto the wet sidewalk. Mr. Moe scurried about, dragging them in from the rain. The grocer looked none the worse for his late-night mission.

When the light changed, I turned left, toward

the alley behind my building. The apartments were built on two levels, with a three-car garage at the rear. I glanced up at my window, over the garage. The draperies were tightly drawn. No one who resembled a cop lurked in the alley.

I pulled the MG behind the trash bins and followed a narrow passageway to Tim O'Riley's apartment at the front of the basement near the furnace room. Tapping on his door, I glanced around nervously. Tim answered right away.

"You!" he exclaimed, regarding me with censorious bloodshot eyes.

"Sssh!" I pushed past him. "Lock the door quick!"

Frowning, he did as I told him. "You're in a whole peck of trouble, you know."

"I know. Where's the cop?"

"In the lobby. Jesus, this place is practically turning into a branch of the morgue. You really kill her?"

"Of course not! They just want to ask me some questions."

Tim looked dubious. "You know something?"

"They think I do."

"How come your boyfriend isn't sticking up for you? He's a cop."

Greg wouldn't stick up for me, not after what I'd done. He'd be more likely to start proceedings to yank my license. I ignored Tim's question and glanced around the apartment. It was smaller than mine, with pale-green cinderblock walls. Tim had decorated with bullfight posters and those hideous

166

paintings on velvet that were the pride of any Mexican border town. On every surface stood souvenirs of his yearly fishing trips to Mexico — mostly ashtrays lifted from cheap motels.

In a moment, Tim flung out his arms resignedly. "Since you're here, you want a brew?"

"I don't think so, not this early. Do you have any coffee?"

"Never touch the stuff, but I think there's some instant. Myself, I'm having a beer. Might as well start the day right."

From his breath, he already had.

I sat down on a rattan chair. When Tim came back, I asked, "What are your chances of going up to my place and getting me a change of clothes?"

"Zilch. That cop would catch on in a flash if I was to stroll through the lobby with an armful of ladies' duds."

"True." I stirred my coffee. "Have you seen Linnea this morning?"

"Nope. She must be sleeping it off. She was really stinko last night when your boyfriend talked to her. Was downright nasty to him, as a matter of fact."

"She's got reason to be." I recalled Linnea's account of her previous meeting with Greg. "Well, I guess I'm stuck with these clothes. Do you think I could wash up?"

There was a knock at the door.

Tim and I stared wide-eyed at one another.

"In the closet," he whispered, yanking me up

and pushing me toward a curtained-off alcove.

I leaped in there and stood, wrapped in the embrace of Tim's only suit.

"Yeah? Who is it?" Tim unlocked the door.

"Me, Gus."

"Come on in. Some commotion around here, huh?"

"I'll say."

"What's up."

"I want to give you something towards next month's rent."

"The rent? I thought you was gonna give the place up."

"Nope." There was a note of pride in his declaration. "I'm staying. I got me a roommate."

"And who might that be?"

"Sebastian, the brush man. He's decided to leave the Blind Center and put in with me."

Tim grunted. "You sure you can afford it?"

"Sure I can!" Gus said indignantly. "I've got plenty of money."

"Okay, then give me some."

"Will fifty hold it until I get the rest?"

"Sure, I'm easy. Let me give you a receipt."

I risked a look through the curtain. Tim rummaged on his cluttered formica table for a receipt book. Gus wandered around the room, reading the inscriptions on the ashtrays.

"Raining like a bastard out there," he commented. "This is the strangest June we've ever had. I got to go over to the Superette in it and get some TV dinners so they'll be defrosted by lunch time."

I suppressed a snort of laughter. Sebastian had been right: Someone would have to teach Gus to cook.

Apparently Tim wasn't much of a hand in the kitchen, either. He merely said, "Getting all settled up there, huh?"

"Sure am. It's a nice place. I never appreciated it when I lived there with Molly. By the way, the funeral's tomorrow. You coming?"

"You bet."

"I hope the rain quits. Folks won't want to drive all the way to Colma if it doesn't." Colma was the necropolis south of the city.

"Of course they will," Tim said, writing laboriously. "Molly had lots of friends."

"Yeah, she did." There was a note of woe in Gus's voice that could have been either for Molly or for his own relatively friendless state. He sidled across the room, glancing over his shoulder at Tim, who had his back turned.

Gus stopped in front of the bookcase by the door. With a final glance at Tim, he reached out and grabbed the nearest ashtray. Quickly, he stuffed it in his jacket pocket.

This time I had to suppress a gasp.

Tim turned. "There you go." He extended the receipt. "See you pay up on time every month — and no wild parties, you hear?" He laughed boisterously.

Gus departed, giggling.

I stepped out of the closet. "Well, that's a surprise. The last I heard, both he and Sebastian were broke."

"Beats me where they're getting it from. And the two of them as roommates — I bet Molly would've had a fit."

"Why?"

"Molly didn't approve of anything Gus did, unless she told him to do it first."

"He's developed an independent attitude rather rapidly." A suspicion formed in my mind. "Tim, you've known both Gus and Molly a long time, right?"

"Since I first took over as manager here, about fifteen years ago. Of course, they lived together back then."

"Then you must remember when she threw him out."

"I sure do. She rented him that room up the hill and moved him lock, stock, and barrel. At first he put up an awful howl, camped out on the front steps for a couple of nights. But once he got settled in up there, he seemed to like it."

"Do you know why she threw him out?"

Tim swigged beer and belched. "Sure. She couldn't take any more."

"Any more what?"

"You don't know?"

"No. Tell me!"

"Gus is a kleptomaniac — one of those folks who steals things and can't help it."

Of course. He had to be.

"Believe me," Tim went on, "it was hard on Molly all those years while she worked at Knudsen's. He'd come in to see her and steal stuff. A couple of times he got caught. She covered up for him and paid them back for the stuff he took. I guess it got to her, though, when she retired and had to be around him all the time. Anyway, she finally lost her temper and gave him the old heave-ho."

I remembered Sebastian asking Gus if he'd taken some brushes off his parka. And Gus's feigned innocence. It was disturbing.

"What's wrong?" Tim asked. "He steal something from you?"

"He may very well have. He did from you."

"Oh, yeah?" He glanced around suspiciously.

"Yes. Next time you see him, you should ask him for your ashtray from the Ensenada Inn."

"Well, I'll be darned. I'll be darned."

When I had washed up and gotten ready to leave, Tim was still shaking his head and looking anxiously at his beloved ashtrays.

19

There were no police cars, unmarked or otherwise, at the Blind Center. That could mean they had already picked up Neverman for questioning in his wife's death. On the other hand, they might not be aware that this was his temporary abode. Either way, I was fairly sure I wouldn't run into him here.

I hurried down the path to the church, keeping close to the shrubbery. The basement was cold and damp, and Neverman's room was deserted. I went in and inspected the butts in the ashtray. They smelled long dead. The bag on the floor felt clammy and unslept-in. Neverman probably hadn't come home last night.

To get a better feel for my prime suspect, I thumbed through the books on the crate. They were from the public library: a thick pictorial on the works of Paul Gauguin, a biography of the same artist, and several travel books on Tahiti. I opened the pictorial to a color plate. It was all there: the bold hues and graceful shapes which Neverman had tried to imitate in his dreadful mural.

Everyone, I thought, had his dream, however improbable. Did Neverman imagine an arty idyll on a tropic beach, bought and paid for with the proceeds of ripped-off gloves and shoelaces? And Clemente — did he see fencing as a way to escape this bureaucratic dumping ground of the maimed and the flawed, where red tape and denials of grants brought frustration and failure?

I shut the book.

The storeroom down the hall was crammed with cartons bearing the names of cosmetics manufacturers, apparel houses, and electronics firms. I found transistor radios and calculators, power tools and paint brushes, cashmere sweaters and crepe pans. I pawed through several cartons of stereo components, a stack of individually packed electric crock pots, and boxes of costume jewelry. All of it undoubtedly was stolen, but Clemente undoubtedly had bogus receipts to deny the fact. Although I stood in a treasure trove of hot merchandise, I might never be able to prove it.

A padlocked door at the back of the room must lead to more loot. I took out my collection of keys and tried the smaller ones in the lock. After a few minutes, it yielded.

The room was wall-to-wall wooden crates. I forced the lid on one and looked inside.

Fat green bottles with red seals. The distinctive packaging of Tanqueray gin. I lifted one and almost dropped it, as Mr. Moe had last night.

This gin had to be part of the two forty-foot containerloads stolen last week from Circle Wharf and Warehouse. It would retail at around four hundred and sixty thousand dollars. Clemente,

Neverman, and Mr. Moe would have invested a maximum of a hundred and fifty thousand dollars for the goods — the one-third of retail value that thieves customarily demanded but seldom got. No matter who they unloaded this gin to, they could easily double that investment.

I stared at the green bottle, pondering Mr. Moe's role in all this.

A good drop for stolen goods was a place where many trucks unloaded cargo. A thief could offload his merchandise, then leave. The fence would be nearby in another truck. If no one resembling the law displayed interest in the hot goods, the fence would merely drive up and take it away to a permanent drop. The temporary drop — on the sidewalk — minimized the contact between thief and fence, thus safeguarding against arrest.

Who would notice if some of the goods delivered to the Albatross Superette were not standard grocery items? And who would pay attention when the Blind Center truck picked them up? And why would anyone become curious about trucks that came and went at the Center, which most likely bought its materials and groceries wholesale?

But how did they expect to move two containerloads of the gin through the little Superette? The thieves at the old ironworks at India Basin would be edgy and demand speed of the operation. Were there other drops in other grocery stores throughout the neighborhood? Was that why the Blind Center van traveled about the Mission District with such regularity, even though Sebastian was the one who actually restocked the racks?

Maybe I'd stumbled onto a network of temporary drops.

The thought was intriguing.

I set down the gin bottle and took out my notebook, where I coped the marks that were stamped on the crates: "Sales Liquor Distributors, Oakland, PO 7786-52-B." It didn't mean much right now, but it would come in handy later. I relocked the room and crept down the hall to the side door. Opening it a crack, I peeked out in time to see Clemente bustle by. I followed at a distance and watched him climb into a cab on Twenty-fourth Street. It pulled away, but was halted by the traffic light. I rushed to my car and started after it.

The cab took Army Street to the freeway. We cruised down the Bayshore, past Candlestick Park and the industrial flatlands of South San Francisco. At the airport, the cab took the off-ramp and swept through the endless construction zone to the departure area of the central terminal.

Clemente was taking a sudden trip, without a suitcase.

I found a parking space in a twenty-minute green zone. If I followed Clemente all the way onto his flight, I would get a hell of a ticket. Still, it would be worth the fine: What better place to interrogate a suspect than at thirty thousand feet, where he couldn't get up and walk out on me?

Clemente left the PSA ticket counter when I

entered the terminal. PSA ran commuter flights up and down the West Coast, with frequent service to Los Angeles. I followed Clemente to the concourse, hanging back until he completed the security check. As I passed through the metal detector, I saw him disappear down the ramp to where the LA flights departed. I snatched my purse from the security man and raced to the gate. Clemente entered the boarding chute to the plane.

Commuter flights did not normally require reservations. "Can I buy a ticket for LA here at the gate?" I asked the attendant, checkbook already out.

"You'll have to purchase it at the desk, up the ramp and to your left."

"Thanks."

I ran up and joined the line of LA-bound passengers. It moved slowly, and the clock showed four minutes to departure time.

"Will we make it?" the woman in front of me asked the ticket agent.

"Don't worry." He glanced at the line and spoke into an intercom. "We've got five more passengers up here."

"Okay, we'll wait," a voice replied.

I made out my check and presented it as soon as I reached the desk. The agent slowly wrote up a ticket.

"I need two pieces of identification, a driver's license and a credit card."

Why hadn't I had enough cash on me? "I don't

have any credit cards. I quit using them."

The agent looked at me as if I were demented. "Not even a gas card?"

"Oh. Gas card. Yes." I pulled it out. "Are you sure I'll make it?"

He switched on the intercom again. "We've got one more lady up here, Bill."

"Okay. We're holding."

Slowly, the agent recorded numbers from my license and credit card onto the check. When he finished, I grabbed them and thrust them into my bag. He held onto the ticket while he punched more numbers into a machine. Apparently my check was acceptable, because he noted a code on it and handed me the ticket.

"Have a nice flight."

"Thanks." I tore down the ramp.

"Going to LA? Hurry up." The attendant ripped off a section of my ticket and waved me through the gate.

I raced along the boarding chute. A second attendant stood at its end, silhouetted against the runway. The plane had pulled away.

"The ticket agent called down to the gate!" I wailed. "He said they'd hold it!"

The man looked unconcerned. "Sorry, lady. He may have told the gate, but the gate didn't tell the plane. There's another flight in fifty-five minutes."

I could have sat down and cried. Or kicked him. Or screamed at the ticket agent. But, remembering my mother's teachings on good conduct in public places, I did none of those things. I merely turned in my ticket, haughtily refusing their offer of a later flight.

"But, ma'am, this ticket is good for an entire year."

"Forget it. I'll never attempt to fly your goddamn airline again."

20

I retreated to the bank of phones near the baggage claim area and called Circle Wharf and Warehouse. After much prodding, their president, a Mr. John Hood, gave me a three-thirty appointment — the earliest he had available — to talk about the gin theft. He sounded extremely wary; doubtless he'd been bothered before by people peddling information.

Beating the meter maid to my car by about twenty seconds, I zipped off toward the freeway. The radio mumbled softly under the hum of my engine, and I turned it up when I caught a familiar name.

". . . Marcus, of SFPD Homicide, said all-points bulletins have been issued for the husband of the deceased. San Francisco private investigator Sharon McCone is also being requested to contact the SFPD. McCone is believed to have reported the crime before fleeing the scene last night. In other local news . . ."

Damn! I snapped off the radio. A "request" was a polite way of saying come in or else. No APB had been issued, but squad cars would be on the alert for me. Quickly I moved into the left lane and headed back around the circle to the parking garage. No sense in going anywhere in my battered old MG, which would easily be spotted by the police.

I left the car in the long-term lot and crossed to the terminal once again. Two and a half hours were mine to kill, but somehow I had to get across the Bay to Alameda. My eyes roved around the terminal and rested on the sign for the SFO helicopter.

Well, why not? I'd never taken a helicopter ride before. Soon I stood in line, waiting to buy a ticket for Oakland Airport.

We lifted off twenty-five minutes later, into a gray, dreary sky. The roar was deafening at first, then softer as the copter gained altitude. I clutched the edges of my seat and peered down through a rain-peppered window as the ground fell away. The ten other passengers were evidently old hands at this exotic form of travel; they read their newspapers, oblivious to their surroundings. Fortunately, they were also oblivious to the bedraggled young woman with the unruly mop of black hair who pressed her nose to the glass and delighted in the rise across the choppy waters of the Bay.

Fugitive from justice enjoys last moments of freedom.

The words, like a caption for a newspaper photo, popped into my head. My spirits took a sudden plunge, and I swallowed hard. A request, I reminded myself, is not the same thing as an arrest warrant. The thought didn't help.

At Oakland Airport, I virtually slunk to the ladies' room, glancing around for official uniforms. Inside one of the stalls I removed the fake driver's license and credit card in the same name that I carried in a compartment of my wallet for just such occasions as this. I was already in so much trouble that one more infraction of the law couldn't worsen it measurably.

Approaching the rental car counters, I chose the one staffed by the youngest, least-experienced-looking clerk. She accepted my identification and credit card without a question. Fifteen minutes later I headed for the Port of Alameda in a green Toyota.

Alameda is an island a stone's throw west of Oakland. I rumbled through the tube under the Bay and onto a main strip lined with fast food stands that served the Naval Air Station. Following Mr. Hood's directions, I drove toward the waterfront.

A line of left-turning semis indicated the access road for Circle Wharf and Warehouse. I waited at the security gate between two hulking, puffing trucks that made me feel like a bug about to be squashed. A guard in a green windbreaker and hardhat directed me to a parking space in front of the Administration Building.

As I locked my car, I looked around for police cars, a habit I had developed to a fine art in the last couple of hours. I hoped fervently that Mr. Hood didn't have a radio in his office or, if he did, that he hadn't been listening to the news. After we talked, I should be able to bargain with the law.

Mr. Hood was an imposing gentleman with an iron-gray crewcut and a lean, weathered face. As he admitted me to his office and settled me on a leather couch, his manner was cordial, but wary. He sat down behind his desk and regarded me thoughtfully.

"One of the reasons I agreed to see you," he said, "was because I've never gotten a look at a female private eye before."

"So now that you have, what do you think?"

"You'd never know, to see you on the street. You look like you could be someone's very efficient secretary. Are you efficient?"

"In my way."

"Are you tough?"

"Pretty tough."

"Know judo? Know how to slap thugs around?"

I couldn't tell if he was baiting me or honestly curious. "I've used judo. As for thugs — I'd rather slap them in jail."

He gave a hoarse, barking laugh. "I like that. You're all right." His eyes sobered. "So what's this about my missing gin?"

"I'm pretty sure I've discovered where it is."

"And what do you want from me? Money?"

"No. Information."

He raised his eyebrows. "You don't want me to hire you? Or pay you to tell me where it is?"

"No. And I can't be positive what I've discovered is yours until you give me some details."

"And then?"

"Then, if it is your missing shipment, I'll tip the FBI. I believe they're the agency that has jurisdiction over this crime."

He nodded, pinching the bridge of his broad nose. Finally he asked, "What's in it for you?"

"I plan to use the discovery to bargain myself out of a tight spot."

"And it wouldn't do me any good to ask what kind of tight spot."

"Right. Of course," I added, "should you or your insurance company see fit to reward me after the recovery of the cargo, I'll leave my card. That way, you'll know where to send the check."

Again, he laughed. "I like your style. Okay, what do you want to know?"

"First, how did the thieves get two full containers out of here in the first place? Your security looks pretty tight."

"It's tight. It's tight twenty-four hours a day, seven days a week. And when a ship's working, it's even tighter. They got those containers out of here the simplest way possible: by presenting what looked like a bona fide delivery order from the steamship line."

"What's a delivery order?"

"Facsimile of the bill of lading. It's our signal from the steamship line that all charges have been paid and the cargo's ready to roll. Take that fellow." He gestured at the window. "Down by the security shack, the driver of a red semi cab was presenting a paper to the guard in the hardhat.

"That fellow," Hood went on, "will show his delivery order to our clerk. If we have the Customs release and the papers are in order, he'll hook up the container and haul it away."

"And, in the case we're talking about, the delivery order only looked genuine."

"Right."

"How'd they fake it?"

He shrugged. "Ladings are customarily made up as ditto masters by the shipper or his forwarder. They're sent to the steamship line, where the appropriate documents are run off. Anybody at any point along the line can run off extra copies of whatever document he wants."

"Surely it would be easy to find out who did it."

"It should be, but we're dealing with extremely clever people. That delivery order was a damned good fake, and the so-called truckers who showed up for the cargo were as cool as they come. It wasn't until the real drivers arrived a few hours later that we realized what had happened. By then, the gin was long gone."

All the way to India Basin, I thought. By day, it was a congested industrial area where no one would notice a couple of extra semis.

"Okay," I said, "if I were to stumble across a lot of Tanqueray gin in an unlikely place, what would I look for to make sure it was this particular shipment?"